Echoes Of The Fireflies: The Citadel

Firefies Of The Heart, Volume 3

Night Intruder

Published by Night Intruder, 2024.

ECHOES OF THE FIREFLIES:THE CITADEL

First edition. October 21, 2024.

Copyright © 2024 Night Intruder.

ISBN: 979-8227216359

Written by Night Intruder.

Table of Contents

For my beloved Anita,

Your unwavering love and support illuminate my path,

inspiring every word I write.

This journey is a reflection of our shared dreams.

Chapter 1: The Night Glade

The Night Glade was alive with a soft, ethereal glow. Thousands of fireflies drifted through the air, their light pulsing in rhythmic patterns that whispered secrets to those who could listen. The bioluminescent plants lining the paths shimmered underfoot, creating a river of pale blue that guided the Luminaires through their duties.

Orion stood at the edge of a clearing, his eyes scanning the sky. The eldest of Evelyn and Lucian's children, he had inherited not only their powers but their responsibilities. As the leader of the new generation of Luminaires, he felt the weight of his lineage every time he stepped into the glade. Tonight was no different. His gaze remained steady, tracking the fireflies as they danced in organized swarms.

"Orion, they're responding to the new tune," Lyra called from deeper within the clearing. Her voice, light and melodic, blended with the soft notes of her flute. She sat cross-legged on a mossy stone, her fingers moving deftly over the instrument. As she played, the fireflies gathered around her, their light forming a spiral that pulsed in time with the melody. "It's almost they are here trying to say something."

Orion frowned. "Be careful, Lyra. Do not push them too much." His tone was serious, but there was a hint of concern in his eyes. He knew his sister's bond with the fireflies was deep, sometimes too deep. "We need to keep things steady."

Lyra glanced up, her expression a mix of curiosity and determination. "I know. But there is something different about them tonight. It is like they want to show us more."

"Or maybe they're just bored," Cassian muttered as he approached from the edge of the glade. The youngest of the trio, his carefree grin contrasted with Orion's stern demeanor. He waved his hand, summoning a small swirl of shadows that danced between the fireflies. The insects scattered momentarily, their light disrupted by his playfulness. "Orion, you worry too much. Not everything is a crisis."

Orion shot him a look. "And you take things too lightly. Our duty is to protect the fireflies, not to toy with them."

Cassian shrugged, his grin fading into an irritated smirk. "Maybe they could use a little fun. Who knows? They might even like it." He let the shadows dissolve and turned away, frustration simmering in his eyes.

Lyra's music shifted, the tune becoming slower, more somber. The fireflies responded immediately, forming intricate patterns that danced through the air like glowing threads weaving an ancient tapestry. Orion's attention sharpened, his eyes following the patterns as they shifted and swirled.

"Wait." Lyra's voice trembled slightly. "They're... they're forming runes." She stopped playing, the flute lowering from her lips as her gaze fixed on the fireflies. "I've never seen them react like this before."

Orion stepped closer, his hand resting on her shoulder. "Let us not push it tonight. We will report this to the Council in the morning. Maybe they will know what it means."

Lyra hesitated but nodded. "Okay. But something feels... off. It is like they are trying to warn us."

Cassian rolled his eyes, trying to mask the hint of worry creeping into his voice. "Or maybe it is just a trick of the light. Come on, let us finish and get back."

Orion watched his brother carefully but said nothing. As Lyra tucked her flute away, the fireflies scattered, their light returning to its usual, gentle glow. But as they made their way out of the clearing,

Orion could not shake the feeling that they had missed something important—something hidden within the flicker of the fireflies' light.

The journey back to the Citadel was quiet, the only sound being the soft rustle of leaves and the hum of the fireflies that still lingered in the air. Orion led the way, his shoulders tense as he scanned the path ahead. Beside him, Lyra walked with her flute tucked under her arm, her eyes distant as she replayed the patterns she had seen in her mind.

Cassian trailed a few steps behind, hands in his pockets, his expression unreadable. He glanced back at the clearing they had left behind, a flicker of curiosity in his eyes. The runes the fireflies had formed were like nothing he had seen before, and the mysterious patterns tugged at his mind.

As they reached the outskirts of the Night Glade, Orion stopped and turned to face his siblings. "Whatever happened back there, we need to stay focused. The Council will know what to do."

Lyra nodded, though doubt lingered in her eyes. "I just wish we knew what they were trying to tell us. It felt urgent, like they needed us to understand."

Cassian smirked, shrugging off her concern. "Or maybe it is nothing. Just another weird thing the fireflies do." His voice was casual, but the intensity in his gaze hinted at more.

Orion's eyes narrowed. "You are too quick to dismiss things, Cassian. One day, you might regret not taking this seriously."

Cassian rolled his eyes, but there was no retort. Instead, he watched as Orion and Lyra continued toward the towering gates of the Citadel, their home, and the heart of the Luminaires' power. He hesitated, glancing back one last time at the trail that had led them here. The fireflies hovered, their glow fading as the night deepened.

He turned to follow his siblings, but a sudden flicker of light caught his attention. A path, faint, and shimmering appeared at the edge of his vision. The fireflies had formed a glowing trail leading deeper into the forest—a trail that had not been there moments ago.

Curiosity sparked in Cassian's eyes. He glanced at Orion and Lyra, now out of sight, and made a quick decision. Silently, he stepped off the path and followed the trail. The light grew brighter as he moved deeper into the woods, the fireflies clustering in a dense, swirling cloud.

When he reached the end of the trail, the fireflies gathered into a tight formation, their glow illuminating a small grove. At its center stood a figure cloaked in shadow. Cassian felt a chill run down his spine, but he did not move. The figure stepped forward, and the fireflies shifted, forming another rune in the air—one that pulsed with a warning glow.

"Curiosity can be a powerful tool, young one," the figure said, its voice low and smooth. "But it can also lead to truths you are not prepared for."

Cassian's eyes narrowed. "Who are you?"

"A friend," the figure replied, the shadows around it shifting like smoke. "Or perhaps an ally, if you are willing to see beyond the rules your family clings to."

Cassian's heart raced, but he forced himself to keep calm. "What do you want?"

The figure tilted its head. "Not much. Just to offer you a glimpse of what lies beyond the limits the Luminaires have set for you. The fireflies are more than just guardians. They hold the power to reshape the world—but only if someone is brave enough to harness it."

Cassian hesitated, his curiosity battling with caution. "And why would you tell me this?"

"Because I see potential in you," the figure said, its voice almost a whisper. "The potential to be more than just a guardian. To be a creator, a shaper of destiny."

The fireflies around them pulsed again, and Cassian felt a pull—a temptation he could not ignore. But before he could respond, the figure vanished, melting into the shadows. The fireflies scattered, their light dimming as the grove fell into darkness.

Cassian stood alone, the weight of the encounter settling on his shoulders. He did not know what the figure wanted, but its words lingered in his mind, stirring questions he could not yet answer.

He turned back, retracing his steps to the path that led to the Citadel. This time, he walked faster, glancing over his shoulder as the shadows crept in. The fireflies had disappeared, leaving him with only his thoughts—and the promise of secrets yet to be uncovered.

Chapter 2: Shadows of Doubt

The Citadel loomed against the night sky, its towers covered in a web of vines that glowed faintly, a reminder of the ancient magic that coursed through its walls. The fireflies fluttered around the entrance, their light illuminating the stone steps that led to the inner chambers where the Luminaires gathered.

Orion pushed open the heavy doors and stepped inside, Lyra following close behind. The warm glow of torches lined the hall, casting long shadows that flickered as they moved. Cassian lagged a few steps behind, his mind still preoccupied with the mysterious figure he had encountered in the grove. He remained silent as they entered the central chamber, where the Council's relics stood on pedestals—a testament to the history of the Luminaires and their mission.

Orion paused, turning to face his siblings. "We will report what happened in the morning. Until then, I want both of you to stay vigilant. Whatever those runes were, we need to understand them before we act."

Lyra nodded, her expression thoughtful. "I will study the patterns again. Maybe there is something in the archives that matches what I saw."

Cassian, however, seemed distant, his eyes fixed on the relics displayed before them. The rogue magician's words echoed in his mind. He felt a strange sense of restlessness, as if the Citadel's walls were closing in around him. "Or we could just wait and see if it happens again," he said, shrugging. "It's not like the fireflies haven't been weird before."

Orion's eyes narrowed. "This is different, Cassian. You saw it yourself. We cannot afford to be careless."

Cassian held his brother's gaze, but something in his expression was guarded, as if he were holding back. "Yeah, sure," he muttered, turning away.

Orion watched him for a moment longer, then sighed. "Get some rest. We will regroup tomorrow." He glanced at Lyra, giving her a nod of encouragement before heading down the corridor to his quarters.

Lyra remained, sensing the tension between her brothers. She approached Cassian, her voice gentle. "What is going on with you? You have been acting strange since we left the glade."

Cassian's eyes flicked to hers, and for a brief moment, she saw the uncertainty there. But then he masked it with a grin. "I am fine, Lyra. Tired, I guess." He gave her a light shove. "Go on, get some sleep."

She did not move, her eyes searching his face. "Cassian, if something happened, you could tell me."

He hesitated, the memory of the shadowy figure flashing in his mind. But he pushed it aside, forcing a smile. "It is nothing. Really." Without another word, he turned and walked down the corridor, disappearing into the shadows.

Lyra watched him go, worry tightening her chest. She knew her brother well enough to recognize when he was hiding something. But she also knew he would not talk until he was ready. With a sigh, she headed to the library, determined to find any information she could about the runes the fireflies had formed.

The library was a vast room, its walls lined with ancient tomes and scrolls that documented the history of the Luminaires and the mysteries of the fireflies. Lyra moved through the aisles, her fingers trailing over the worn spines as she searched for anything that might hold the answers she sought.

As she read, the hours slipped by. She found references to the fireflies' connection to light and healing, but nothing that explained the runes she had seen. Frustration began to build, and she closed the book in front of her with a sigh. "What are you trying to tell me?" she whispered, her gaze drifting to the candle flickering beside her.

Suddenly, the light from the candle shifted, casting a strange shadow on the wall. Lyra's heart skipped a beat as the shadows formed a familiar shape—the same rune she had seen in the glade. She stood, her pulse quickening. The shadow moved again, morphing into a different symbol, one that pulsed with a rhythm that matched her music.

The fireflies' light, she realized, was not just reacting to her melody. It was communicating.

Determined, she grabbed her flute and began to play, her fingers moving swiftly as she matched the rhythm of the shadow. The candlelight flickered, and the shadow expanded, revealing more runes, forming a sequence. Lyra's eyes widened as she recognized one of the symbols—it was the same mark she had seen in an old scroll, a warning sign used by the Luminaires' ancestors.

She stopped playing, the realization hitting her. The fireflies were trying to warn them of an ancient threat, one that had been long forgotten.

Meanwhile, Cassian stood in the darkness of his room, staring at the ceiling. His encounter with the rogue magician had left him with more questions than answers. The figure's words echoed in his mind: The fireflies are more than just guardians. They hold the power to reshape the world.

He clenched his fists, frustration boiling within him. The Luminaires had trained them to protect the fireflies, to follow the rules passed down for generations. But what if the rules were holding them back? What if there was more to their power—more that could be done if only someone had the courage to explore it?

A knock at his door snapped him out of his thoughts. He opened it to find the same shadowy figure standing in the doorway, the fireflies' light glinting off his hood.

"Cassian," the figure said, its voice a whisper. "Have you considered my offer?"

Cassian's heart raced. "How did you get in here?"

The figure stepped inside, the shadows shifting around him. "The fireflies and I have an understanding. They show me what I need to see—and tonight, they brought me to you."

Cassian felt a mix of fear and excitement. "What do you want from me?"

The rogue magician smiled, his eyes glinting. "Not much. Just your trust. Let me show you what the fireflies are truly capable of."

Cassian hesitated, glancing down the hallway. Orion and Lyra were still in the Citadel, and he knew they would never approve of him meeting with this stranger. But the promise of knowledge—of power—was too tempting to resist.

"Fine," he said, his voice barely a whisper. "But no tricks."

"Of course," the magician replied, his smile widening. "I have much to teach you, Cassian. And together, we can unlock the fireflies' true potential."

Cassian's eyes narrowed, but he nodded. "Lead the way."

As they slipped into the shadows, Cassian felt a thrill of excitement. For the first time, he was taking control—making his own choice, even if it meant defying everything he had been taught.

But deep down, a small voice whispered that he was stepping into a darkness he might never escape.

Chapter 3: The Ancient Texts

Morning broke over the Citadel, casting rays of golden light through the tall, arched windows of the council chamber. The Luminaires gathered, their voices low as they shared the reports from their nightly patrols. Orion, standing at the front with his arms crossed, waited for the others to finish before stepping forward.

"The fireflies formed runes last night—something we've never seen before," he announced. His tone was calm but carried an edge of urgency. "I believe they were trying to send us a message."

The room fell silent as the council members exchanged glances. A murmur of concern rippled through the chamber, and an elder Luminaire, Master Eryndor, nodded slowly. "The runes are a rare occurrence. It has been many generations since they last appeared."

Lyra, seated beside Orion, leaned forward. "I have been researching the archives, but I have not found anything that matches the runes we saw. If there is any record of this, it is buried deep."

Master Eryndor's eyes darkened. "There are secrets even our archives do not hold, Lyra. The runes are tied to an ancient power—one that predates the founding of the Luminaires."

Before Orion could respond, Cassian, standing at the back of the room, spoke up. "You mean the power that my mother, Evelyn, sacrificed everything for when she founded the Luminaires?"

The council members turned to face him, and a tense silence filled the chamber. Cassian's eyes were sharp, and there was a note of defiance in his voice. "She gave up her life to create this order and protect the fireflies. She believed in the balance they could bring, but now, you act like you are afraid of their power."

Master Eryndor's expression softened. "Cassian, your mother's legacy is honored every day we carry out our duties. But she also knew the risks—knew that some forces should remain dormant."

Cassian's gaze remained locked on the elder. "Or maybe she understood that power should not be feared or hidden away. Maybe she knew it could be used for more."

Orion stepped in, placing a hand on Cassian's shoulder. "We all respect what she did, Cassian. But right now, we need to understand what the fireflies are trying to tell us."

Cassian shrugged off his brother's hand. "I'm just saying, maybe it's time the council stopped hiding behind old traditions and started remembering what she stood for." His voice was cold as he turned and left the chamber, leaving a heavy silence in his wake.

Orion sighed as he watched Cassian Walk away, worry creasing his brow. Lyra remained seated, her eyes fixed on the table. She knew Cassian's frustration ran deep, but she also sensed something more—a restlessness that had grown since the fireflies had formed the runes.

That night, the siblings returned to the Night Glade. The air was crisp, and the fireflies hovered in clusters, their glow illuminating the familiar paths. Lyra pulled out her flute and began to play, her melody echoing softly through the trees. As the music filled the glade, the fireflies started to form patterns once again, their light shifting and weaving into the runes they had seen before.

Orion watched intently, his eyes tracing the shapes as they appeared. "That one—" he pointed to a rune that pulsed with a soft, blue light, "—it matches a symbol from the ancient texts I found in the library."

Lyra paused, lowering her flute. "What does it mean?"

"It's a warning," Orion replied, his expression grim. "A sign that the balance of light and darkness is being threatened."

Cassian's eyes flicked to the rune, but his thoughts were elsewhere. The rogue magician's words echoed in his thoughts: The fireflies hold the power to reshape the world. If this Lightbringer was as powerful as the council claimed, it was no wonder the magician wanted to unlock its secrets.

As they continued their patrol, Lyra's music grew softer, and the fireflies' patterns shifted, revealing a new rune—one that Cassian recognized immediately. It was the same symbol the rogue magician had shown him in the grove. His pulse quickened as the fireflies pulsed, their light forming the shape over and over again.

He felt a pull, an Invisible thread tugging at his heart. The fireflies were trying to show him something—something only he could see. "Lyra, keep playing," he urged, his voice low.

Orion shot him a look of caution. "What is it, Cassian?"

But Cassian ignored him, stepping closer to the glowing swarm. The runes shifted again, forming a pattern that stretched across the glade, leading into the depths of the forest. The fireflies clustered into a tight formation, their light brighter than before.

Without waiting for his siblings, Cassian followed the trail. Orion called out, but Cassian was already moving through the trees, his eyes fixed on the path ahead. He could hear Lyra's music fading behind him, but the pull of the fireflies was stronger than anything he had felt before.

The trail led him to a small, hidden clearing surrounded by towering trees. The fireflies hovered above, illuminating the figure standing at the center. The rogue magician's face was hidden beneath a hood, but his eyes glinted as he watched Cassian approach.

"You came," the magician said, his voice a whisper that seemed to echo through the glade. "I knew you would."

Cassian's heart pounded, but he forced himself to stand his ground. "What do you want?"

The magician gestured to the fireflies, their light reflecting off his cloak. "I want to show you the truth—the truth your family has kept hidden from you. The fireflies are not just guardians. They are keys, and with them, we can unlock a power greater than you have ever imagined."

Cassian felt a rush of excitement and fear. "And why should I trust you?"

The magician smiled, and the shadows around him shifted. "Because you seek the truth, Cassian. You have always felt that there is more to the world than the limits the Luminaires set for you. Let me show you what lies beyond those limits."

Cassian hesitated, glancing back the way he came. He knew Orion and Lyra would never approve of this, but something in the magician's voice resonated with him. The fireflies' light pulsed, matching the rhythm of his heartbeat.

"All right," he said finally. "Show me."

The magician extended his hand, and Cassian felt a surge of energy as he took it. The fireflies circled them, their light forming a cocoon that lifted them off the ground. Cassian's eyes widened as the world around him blurred, and for a moment, he felt as if he were floating in a sea of stars.

When the light faded, they stood in a cavern, its walls covered in glowing runes. Cassian's breath caught in his throat as he realized where they were. The ancient temple—the one from the stories his parents had told him.

"This is where it begins," the rogue magician said. "The temple of the Lightbringer. And this—" he gestured to the fireflies as they swirled around a massive stone altar, "—is where the truth has been hidden."

Cassian stared at the altar, the fireflies' light reflecting off its surface. The runes carved into the stone glowed faintly, their patterns matching those he had seen in the glade. The rogue magician's words echoed in his mind: The fireflies are more than just guardians. They hold the power to reshape the world.

He felt a thrill of excitement and fear. "What do we do?"

The magician's smile widened. "We begin the ritual."

Chapter 4: A Melody in the Dark

The temple's walls echoed with a haunting silence, the air thick with the energy of ancient magic. Cassian stood before the massive stone altar, the fireflies circling above, their glow casting eerie shadows that danced along the runes carved into the stone. The rogue magician's presence felt like a shadow looming behind him, and despite the thrill of the moment, a voice deep within Cassian's mind urged caution.

"The fireflies respond to those who are worthy," the rogue magician said, his voice soft but filled with a persuasive power. "Your mother understood that. She believed in the power they held, and she sacrificed everything to protect it. But she never unlocked their full potential. We can, Cassian. We can finish what she started."

Cassian's heart pounded in his chest. The fireflies pulsed in time with his heartbeat, and he felt their energy flowing through him. "And what do you want me to do?"

The magician stepped closer, his eyes glinting in the firefly light. "Play your part. The runes need to be activated. With your connection to the fireflies and my guidance, we can unleash the power within this temple."

Cassian's hand hovered over the runes, uncertainty flickering in his eyes. His mother's legacy felt like a weight on his shoulders, but the temptation to prove himself, to be more than just a guardian, was overpowering. "If I do this..., will it really show me the truth?"

The magician's smile was cold. "It will show you everything."

Before Cassian could respond, the fireflies brightened, and a sharp ringing sound filled the air. He turned, his eyes narrowing as the runes glowed with an intensity that matched the fireflies' light. "What's happening?"

The magician's smile widened. "The fireflies recognize your power. They are opening the path."

Elsewhere in the Citadel, Orion paced the library, his brow furrowed as he pored over the ancient texts. Lyra sat across from him, her eyes scanning the pages for any reference to the symbols they had seen. "There's nothing," she said, her frustration evident. "We've searched everything."

Orion sighed, running a hand through his hair. "We are missing something. The council is holding back—there is more to this than they are telling us."

Lyra's fingers tightened around the edge of the book. "And Cassian... he has been acting strange ever since the runes appeared. I cannot shake the feeling that he knows more than he is letting on."

Orion looked up, his eyes serious. "We need to keep an eye on him. If he is involved with this magician, he could be in danger."

Lyra nodded, but there was a hesitation in her eyes. "Orion, what if he is right? What if we have been too focused on the rules, on what the council says, and we are missing something important?"

Orion's expression softened, and he reached out to squeeze her hand. "I know it is hard to question everything we have been taught, but we have to be careful. Whatever is happening with the fireflies, it is powerful—and dangerous. We cannot risk Cassian getting caught up in something that could destroy everything our mother built."

Lyra's gaze dropped to the table, the weight of their situation settling on her. "We have to find him, Orion. Before it is too late."

In the Night Glade, the fireflies danced around Lyra as she played her flute, her melody carrying through the still air. She let the music flow, her eyes closed as she focused on the rhythm of the fireflies' light.

The patterns began to shift, and she felt their energy pulling her deeper into their world.

Suddenly, the fireflies' glow intensified, and a new rune appeared in the air—a symbol she had never seen before. Lyra's fingers stumbled on the flute, but she regained her focus, playing the melody that matched the fireflies' rhythm. The rune pulsed, and she felt a strange warmth spreading through her chest.

As the music continued, the fireflies' patterns expanded, forming a path through the glade. Lyra's eyes widened as the path illuminated a hidden trail leading into the depths of the forest. She had never seen the fireflies react this way before, and a thrill of both fear and excitement coursed through her.

Orion appeared at her side, his eyes fixed on the glowing path. "What is it?"

"I don't know," Lyra replied, her voice barely above a whisper. "But the fireflies... they're showing us something."

Orion's gaze remained steady as he watched the fireflies swirl. "We need to follow it."

They moved together, the fireflies guiding them deeper into the forest. The path led to a small grove, the same grove Cassian had been led to before. As they stepped inside, Lyra felt a chill run down her spine. The fireflies formed a circle, and in the center, a shadowy figure stood waiting.

"Welcome," the rogue magician said, his voice carrying a hint of amusement. "I've been expecting you."

Orion's hand went to the hilt of his blade, but Lyra placed a hand on his arm, stopping him. "What do you want?" she asked, her voice steady.

The magician's smile was cold. "I want to show you the truth—about your mother, about the fireflies, and about the power you were meant to wield."

Orion's grip tightened, but Lyra's eyes remained locked on the magician's. "And why should we believe you?"

"Because" the magician said, stepping closer, "the council has lied to you. They have hidden the truth for generations, afraid of the power your mother tried to unlock. But you, Lyra—you have the gift to awaken it. All you need to do is trust me."

Lyra's heart pounded as she felt the fireflies' energy pulling her toward the magician. The temptation to know more, to uncover the secrets her mother had sacrificed so much for, was overwhelming. But a part of her hesitated, the voice of caution she had inherited from her mother whispering in her mind.

Orion stepped forward, his voice firm. "We do not need your lies. We protect the fireflies, and we protect the balance. Whatever you are after, you will not find it with us."

The rogue magician's smile faded, his eyes turning cold. "Very well. But know this—when the time comes, the fireflies will choose the one who is worthy. And when they do, it will be too late for you to stop it."

As the fireflies' light dimmed, the magician vanished into the shadows, leaving the siblings alone in the grove. Lyra's hands trembled as she lowered her flute, and she felt the weight of his words hanging in the air.

Orion placed a hand on her shoulder. "Are you all, right?"

She nodded, though doubt lingered in her eyes. "We have to find Cassian. I think... I think he has already made his choice."

Orion's expression darkened. "Then we will bring him back. No matter what it takes."

As they left the grove, the fireflies' light guided their way, but Lyra's heart was heavy. She could feel the balance shifting, the magic of the fireflies pulling them toward a destiny they could not yet see. And for the first time, she feared that the choices they made might not be enough to save them all.

Chapter 5: The Shattered Veil

The wind howled through the forest as the night deepened, carrying with it the whispers of unseen forces. Orion and Lyra moved swiftly through the glade, the fireflies' glow lighting their path as they searched for any sign of Cassian. The trees loomed like silent sentinels, and the air was thick with tension, as if the forest itself sensed the coming storm.

Orion's grip tightened around the hilt of his blade as he scanned the shadows. "He has to be close. The fireflies would not guide us this far if they did not know where he was."

Lyra nodded, her eyes scanning the darkness. "I can feel his presence. It is faint, but he is somewhere near." She played a soft note on her flute, the melody echoing through the trees and coaxing the fireflies to form patterns that led them deeper into the woods.

As they followed the glowing trail, Lyra's heart pounded. She could feel the energy of the fireflies pulsing around them, more intense than she had ever felt before. The runes she had seen in the glade flashed in her mind, and a sense of urgency gripped her. "Orion, what if the fireflies are leading us to something else—something they want us to see?"

Orion's eyes flicked to her, his expression serious. "Then we will face it together. But we need to find Cassian first."

Just as he spoke, the fireflies' light flared, and the ground beneath them trembled. Lyra stumbled, catching herself against a tree as the forest seemed to shudder. "What's happening?"

Orion's gaze shot upward, and his eyes widened as he saw the sky splitting open, a crack of darkness tearing through the night. The fireflies swarmed, their light dimming as they clustered around the rift that had formed above the glade. "The Shattered Veil," he whispered. "it's opening."

Lyra's eyes were wide with fear. "But it has been sealed for generations—since before the Luminaires were founded. How is it possible?"

Before Orion could answer, a voice echoed through the clearing—a familiar, taunting voice. "Because someone was brave enough to unlock its power."

Orion and Lyra turned to see Cassian standing at the edge of the glade, the rogue magician beside him. Cassian's eyes glowed with an intensity they had never seen before, and the fireflies clustered around him, their light casting long shadows across the ground.

"Cassian, what are you doing?" Orion's voice was tight with a mix of fear and anger. "You know what the Shattered Veil is—what it can unleash."

Cassian's gaze flicked between his siblings, a look of conflict flashing in his eyes. But he remained still, his expression hardening. "What if the council has been lying to us? What if the fireflies are not just here to maintain balance, but to show us what lies beyond?"

The rogue magician's smile was cold. "Your mother knew the power of the fireflies, but she chose to seal it away, to keep it from those who might have used it to change the world. You do not have to make the same mistake, Cassian."

Lyra stepped forward, her hand outstretched. "Cassian, please. This is not what Mother would have wanted. She sacrificed everything to protect the balance. Do not let this magician twist her legacy."

Cassian's eyes softened for a moment, but the rogue magician's hand tightened on his shoulder. "Your mother's legacy is a cage,

Cassian. You have the chance to set the fireflies free—to let them fulfill their true purpose."

Orion drew his blade, his voice low and filled with warning. "Let him go. The fireflies belong to all of us, and their power is not yours to control."

The rogue magician laughed, his voice echoing through the glade. "It is too late, Luminaire. The Veil is opening, and nothing you do can stop it."

At his words, the crack in the sky widened, and a wave of darkness surged through the forest. The fireflies scattered, their light flickering as shadows spilled from the rift, taking shape as twisted creatures with glowing eyes. Lyra's flute fell silent, and her hands trembled as she gripped it tightly.

"Orion, what do we do?" she whispered, her voice laced with fear.

Orion's jaw clenched. "We fight."

The shadow creatures lunged, their forms shifting as they attacked. Orion moved with swift precision, his blade slicing through the darkness as he defended Lyra. The fireflies swarmed around them, their light pushing back the shadows, but the creatures kept coming, their numbers growing with each passing moment.

Lyra raised her flute, and a melody poured from its silver body—a song of light that resonated with the fireflies' glow. The creatures flinched, their forms faltering as the music filled the glade. The fireflies responded, their light brightening as they formed a protective barrier around the siblings.

Cassian watched, his expression conflicted as his siblings fought to hold back the darkness. The rogue magician's voice whispered in his ear, urging him forward. "This is the power you could wield, Cassian. The power to reshape the world."

Cassian hesitated, his eyes locked on Lyra as she played. Her music, filled with determination and hope, tugged at something deep within him. He saw the pain in her eyes—the fear of losing him—and for a moment, he faltered.

"Cassian, please!" Lyra's voice cut through the chaos, her eyes pleading. "Come back to us. Do not let him use you."

Cassian's hands trembled as he felt the fireflies' energy coursing through him. The shadows called to him, tempting him with promises of power and freedom. But Lyra's melody, filled with the echoes of their mother's legacy, was stronger.

He stepped back, pulling away from the rogue magician's grasp. "No... this isn't right."

The rogue magician's eyes flared with anger, and he raised his hand, summoning the shadows to surround Cassian. "You could have been great, but instead, you choose to cling to weakness."

Orion rushed forward, his blade slicing through the shadows as he reached for Cassian. "We are family. We protect each other—no matter what."

As the siblings stood united, the fireflies' light intensified, pushing back the shadows, and sealing the rift in the sky. The creatures howled as they were pulled back into the Veil, their forms dissipating into the night. The forest fell silent, and the fireflies hovered, their light gentle once more.

Cassian's shoulders slumped, his face a mask of guilt. "I am sorry... I thought I was doing the right thing."

Lyra placed a hand on his arm, her eyes filled with relief. "You came back. That is what matters."

Orion sheathed his blade, his expression softening. "We will face this together. Whatever the fireflies are trying to show us, we will find the truth—together."

The rogue magician's figure faded into the shadows, his voice a whisper that lingered in the air. "You have made your choice, but the fireflies will choose their path. And when they do, you will have to decide where you stand."

As the fireflies' light guided them back through the forest, Cassian felt the weight of his decision settle on his shoulders. The fireflies still pulsed with energy, their patterns shifting in ways he did not yet understand. But for the first time, he knew he did not have to face it alone.

Orion, Lyra, and Cassian walked side by side, their bond stronger than ever. Whatever lay ahead, they would face it together—just as their mother had always intended.

Chapter 6: The Betrayal

The Citadel's stone walls felt colder than usual as the siblings returned, the echoes of their footsteps filling the grand halls. The fireflies that usually lit the way seemed dimmer, their glow a mere flicker compared to the light that had once danced so freely. Orion led the way, his face set in a mask of determination, while Lyra and Cassian followed, the weight of their recent encounter hanging between them.

As they approached the council chamber, Lyra glanced at Cassian. His expression was distant, his gaze fixed on the floor. "Are you all, right?" she whispered, worry lacing her voice.

Cassian did not respond immediately. When he finally spoke, his voice was quiet. "I am fine. I just... need time to think."

Lyra's eyes softened, but she said nothing more as they entered the chamber. The council members were already gathered, their expressions grave as they awaited the siblings' report. Master Eryndor, the eldest of the Luminaires, raised his hand in silence as Orion stepped forward.

"We encountered the rogue magician again," Orion began. "He's manipulating the fireflies, using their power to open the Shattered Veil."

A murmur of concern rippled through the chamber. Master Eryndor's brow furrowed. "The Shattered Veil has been sealed for generations. If he has found a way to open it, the balance we have fought to protect is in grave danger."

Orion's eyes flashed with frustration. "And why weren't we told about this? The council has kept too many secrets—secrets that are now threatening everything we stand for."

The room fell silent. Lyra's gaze darted between the council members, her expression one of confusion and betrayal. "We need to know the truth," she said. "The fireflies are trying to tell us something, but we don't have all the pieces."

Master Eryndor hesitated, his eyes lingering on Cassian before returning to Orion and Lyra. "There are some truths that even the Luminaires have sworn to protect. Your mother, Evelyn, was one of the few who understood the full extent of the fireflies' power. She sacrificed herself to seal the Veil and protect our world from the darkness beyond."

Cassian's eyes darkened as he finally spoke. "You keep talking about her sacrifice, but all I see is the council's fear. You have turned her legacy into a cage, keeping the fireflies' power locked away."

Orion shot him a warning look, but Cassian continued, his voice rising. "Maybe the rogue magician is right. Maybe the fireflies are meant for more than just maintaining a balance. Maybe they could change everything if we stopped being afraid."

The council members exchanged uneasy glances, but Master Eryndor's expression remained calm. "Cassian, the fireflies' power is not something to be taken lightly. It is a force that must be controlled, or it could bring about chaos."

Cassian's hands clenched at his sides. "Or maybe it could bring something better."

Lyra reached for his arm, her voice pleading. "Cassian, please. We are in this together. Do not let him twist your mind."

Cassian pulled away, his expression conflicted. "I am not sure who is twisting what anymore. All I know is that I am tired of being kept in the dark."

Orion stepped forward, his voice firm. "Cassian, whatever the truth is, we need to face it together. That is what Mother would have wanted."

Cassian's eyes met Orion's, and for a moment, it seemed like he might relent. But the tension in his shoulders remained. "I need space. I cannot think clearly with everyone telling me what to do."

Before Orion or Lyra could respond, Cassian turned and left the chamber, the doors closing with a heavy thud behind him.

The night air was cold as Cassian stood alone on the Citadel's balcony, his thoughts racing. The rogue magician's words echoed in his mind: The fireflies are more than just guardians. They are the key to reshaping the world.

A flicker of light appeared in the corner of his vision, and he turned to see the rogue magician stepping out of the shadows. "I knew you'd come," Cassian said, his voice tight with a mix of anger and frustration.

The magician's eyes glinted in the firefly light. "You have the potential to see beyond the limits your family has set for you. But you have to decide if you are ready to embrace it."

Cassian's hands trembled as he faced the magician. "They keep talking about Mother's sacrifice, but all they do is hide behind her name. She gave up everything for the Luminaires, and all they do is live in fear."

The rogue magician's smile was cold. "Fear has always been their weapon. But you, Cassian, have the power to break free from that fear. To use the fireflies' light as it was meant to be used."

Cassian's eyes burned with a mix of anger and longing. "What do I have to do?"

The magician extended his hand. "Trust me, and together, we will unlock the true potential of the fireflies. But you must be willing to let go of the lies you have been told."

Cassian hesitated, glancing back at the Citadel, where his siblings and the council remained. The weight of their expectations felt like chains holding him back, while the promise of freedom and power beckoned from the shadows.

He took the magician's hand, a sense of finality settling over him. "I'm ready."

Chapter 7: Whispers of the Past

The moon hung high in the sky, casting silver light over the Citadel. The corridors were quiet, the shadows long and still. Orion and Lyra moved swiftly, their footsteps muffled as they approached the entrance to the restricted archives. The heavy wooden doors loomed before them, locked by magic, and guarded by ancient wards.

Orion whispered a spell, his hand hovering over the rune etched into the door. The fireflies that accompanied them flitted around his fingers, their light merging with the soft glow of his magic. Slowly, the door creaked open, revealing a spiral staircase that descended into darkness.

Lyra gripped her flute tightly as she followed Orion down the stairs, her eyes scanning the walls for any sign of danger. "Are you sure this is a good idea?" she whispered.

Orion glanced back, his expression determined. "It is the only way. If the council will not tell us the truth, we will find it ourselves."

The air grew colder as they descended, the stone walls damp and covered in moss. The fireflies illuminated the narrow steps, guiding them until they reached the bottom. A large, iron door blocked their path, its surface inscribed with ancient runes that pulsed faintly.

Lyra raised her flute and played a soft, resonant note that echoed through the chamber. The runes on the door glowed in response, their light flickering as the fireflies hovered close. Orion placed his hand against the door, and the runes shifted, rearranging themselves into a pattern he recognized from the texts.

"It's a seal," he muttered. "A barrier to keep out anyone who isn't meant to be here."

Lyra's eyes met his, a spark of determination in her gaze. "Then let's break it."

Together, they worked to undo the seal. Lyra's music wove through the air, harmonizing with the fireflies' light as Orion chanted the incantation he had memorized from the ancient scrolls. The runes pulsed and then, one by one, they dimmed and faded. The door creaked open, revealing a hidden chamber lined with shelves of dusty tomes and relics.

Lyra's breath caught in her throat as they stepped inside. "This must be it—the records they don't want anyone to see."

Orion nodded, his eyes scanning the shelves. "We need to find anything related to the fireflies and the Lightbringer."

They split up, each searching through the old texts. The fireflies glowed brightly, their light illuminating passages written in faded ink. As Lyra pulled a large, leather-bound tome from the shelf, a piece of parchment slipped out and fluttered to the ground.

She picked it up, her eyes widening as she read the ancient script. "Orion, look at this."

Orion joined her, his gaze falling on the parchment. The symbol at the top matched the runes they had seen in the Night Glade. "It's a map," he whispered, tracing the lines that connected various points marked with firefly patterns. "A map of the places where the fireflies have gathered for centuries."

Lyra's fingers trembled as she flipped through the pages of the book. "And here—these are notes about the Lightbringer ritual. It says that the fireflies' power was meant to be used to maintain balance, but there is also a warning. If the ritual is performed incorrectly, it could unleash chaos."

Orion's face darkened. "The rogue magician must be trying to complete the ritual. He is using Cassian because of his connection to the fireflies."

Lyra's voice was urgent. "We have to stop him. If he succeeds, the fireflies' power could be twisted into something destructive."

Orion nodded, a fierce determination in his eyes. "Then we find Cassian, and we make sure he knows the truth."

Meanwhile, Cassian stood at the edge of a cliff overlooking the vast expanse of the Night Glade. The rogue magician stood beside him, his cloak billowing in the wind. The fireflies swirled around them, their light casting eerie shadows that danced over the rocky terrain.

Cassian's thoughts were a whirlwind as he tried to reconcile everything, he had been taught with what he was now seeing. The magician had shown him glimpses of the fireflies' true power—how their light could be harnessed to create and reshape, to bend reality itself. But he could not shake the memory of his siblings' faces, the fear and doubt in their eyes.

"You hesitate," the rogue magician said, his voice low. "You fear the unknown, but the fireflies do not. They seek those who are willing to unlock their potential."

Cassian's hands balled into fists. "I am not afraid of their power. I just want to know if what you are saying is true."

The magician's smile was cold, his eyes gleaming. "It is the council who fears the truth. They sealed the Lightbringer ritual to prevent others from discovering the fireflies' true purpose. But your mother... she knew."

Cassian's breath caught. "What do you mean?"

The magician stepped closer, his voice a whisper. "She attempted the ritual once, long ago. But she was betrayed—by those she trusted most."

Cassian's heart pounded as the fireflies pulsed around them. "You're lying."

The rogue magician's expression softened, and for a moment, there was no malice in his eyes, only truth. "Search your memories. You have always felt it, haven't you? The sense that there was more to your mother's story than what you were told."

Cassian turned away, his gaze fixed on the fireflies as they danced through the air. The rogue magician's words echoed in his mind, stirring doubts he had long buried. "If she tried the ritual and failed... what makes you think we can succeed?"

The magician placed a hand on Cassian's shoulder. "Because this time, we have the key—the fireflies recognize you, Cassian. They know your power. With your connection and my knowledge, we can complete what your mother started."

Cassian's eyes burned with a mix of anger and longing. "And if it goes wrong?"

The magician's grip tightened. "We must be willing to take risks if we want to change the world. But you have to choose—will you follow the path your mother set, or will you cling to the lies of those who betrayed her?"

Cassian's jaw clenched. The fireflies' light intensified, and he felt their energy coursing through him. "I will do it. But if you are lying... you will pay."

The magician's smile returned, cold and triumphant. "Then we begin the ritual at dawn."

Chapter 7: Whispers of the Past

The moon hung high in the sky, casting silver light over the Citadel. The corridors were quiet, the shadows long and still. Orion and Lyra moved swiftly, their footsteps muffled as they approached the entrance to the restricted archives. The heavy wooden doors loomed before them, locked by magic, and guarded by ancient wards.

Orion whispered a spell, his hand hovering over the rune etched into the door. The fireflies that accompanied them flitted around his fingers, their light merging with the soft glow of his magic. Slowly, the door creaked open, revealing a spiral staircase that descended into darkness.

Lyra gripped her flute tightly as she followed Orion down the stairs, her eyes scanning the walls for any sign of danger. "Are you sure this is a good idea?" she whispered.

Orion glanced back, his expression determined. "It is the only way. If the council will not tell us the truth, we will find it ourselves."

The air grew colder as they descended, the stone walls damp and covered in moss. The fireflies illuminated the narrow steps, guiding them until they reached the bottom. A large, iron door blocked their path, its surface inscribed with ancient runes that pulsed faintly.

Lyra raised her flute and played a soft, resonant note that echoed through the chamber. The runes on the door glowed in response, their light flickering as the fireflies hovered close. Orion placed his hand against the door, and the runes shifted, rearranging themselves into a pattern he recognized from the texts.

"It's a seal," he muttered. "A barrier to keep out anyone who isn't meant to be here."

Lyra's eyes met his, a spark of determination in her gaze. "Then let's break it."

Together, they worked to undo the seal. Lyra's music wove through the air, harmonizing with the fireflies' light as Orion chanted the incantation he had memorized from the ancient scrolls. The runes pulsed and then, one by one, they dimmed and faded. The door creaked open, revealing a hidden chamber lined with shelves of dusty tomes and relics.

Lyra's breath caught in her throat as they stepped inside. "This must be it—the records they don't want anyone to see."

Orion nodded, his eyes scanning the shelves. "We need to find anything related to the fireflies and the Lightbringer."

They split up, each searching through the old texts. The fireflies glowed brightly, their light illuminating passages written in faded ink. As Lyra pulled a large, leather-bound tome from the shelf, a piece of parchment slipped out and fluttered to the ground.

She picked it up, her eyes widening as she read the ancient script. "Orion, look at this."

Orion joined her, his gaze falling on the parchment. The symbol at the top matched the runes they had seen in the Night Glade. "It's a map," he whispered, tracing the lines that connected various points marked with firefly patterns. "A map of the places where the fireflies have gathered for centuries."

Lyra's fingers trembled as she flipped through the pages of the book. "And here—these are notes about the Lightbringer ritual. It says that the fireflies' power was meant to be used to maintain balance, but there is also a warning. If the ritual is performed incorrectly, it could unleash chaos."

Orion's face darkened. "The rogue magician must be trying to complete the ritual. He is using Cassian because of his connection to the fireflies."

Lyra's voice was urgent. "We have to stop him. If he succeeds, the fireflies' power could be twisted into something destructive."

Orion nodded, a fierce determination in his eyes. "Then we find Cassian, and we make sure he knows the truth."

Meanwhile, Cassian stood at the edge of a cliff overlooking the vast expanse of the Night Glade. The rogue magician stood beside him, his cloak billowing in the wind. The fireflies swirled around them, their light casting eerie shadows that danced over the rocky terrain.

Cassian's thoughts were a whirlwind as he tried to reconcile everything, he had been taught with what he was now seeing. The magician had shown him glimpses of the fireflies' true power—how their light could be harnessed to create and reshape, to bend reality itself. But he could not shake the memory of his siblings' faces, the fear and doubt in their eyes.

"You hesitate," the rogue magician said, his voice low. "You fear the unknown, but the fireflies do not. They seek those who are willing to unlock their potential."

Cassian's hands balled into fists. "I am not afraid of their power. I just want to know if what you are saying is true."

The magician's smile was cold, his eyes gleaming. "It is the council who fears the truth. They sealed the Lightbringer ritual to prevent others from discovering the fireflies' true purpose. But your mother... she knew."

Cassian's breath caught. "What do you mean?"

The magician stepped closer, his voice a whisper. "She attempted the ritual once, long ago. But she was betrayed—by those she trusted most."

Cassian's heart pounded as the fireflies pulsed around them. "You're lying."

The rogue magician's expression softened, and for a moment, there was no malice in his eyes, only truth. "Search your memories. You have always felt it, haven't you? The sense that there was more to your mother's story than what you were told."

Cassian turned away, his gaze fixed on the fireflies as they danced through the air. The rogue magician's words echoed in his mind, stirring doubts he had long buried. "If she tried the ritual and failed... what makes you think we can succeed?"

The magician placed a hand on Cassian's shoulder. "Because this time, we have the key—the fireflies recognize you, Cassian. They know your power. With your connection and my knowledge, we can complete what your mother started."

Cassian's eyes burned with a mix of anger and longing. "And if it goes wrong?"

The magician's grip tightened. "We must be willing to take risks if we want to change the world. But you have to choose—will you follow the path your mother set, or will you cling to the lies of those who betrayed her?"

Cassian's jaw clenched. The fireflies' light intensified, and he felt their energy coursing through him. "I will do it. But if you are lying... you will pay."

The magician's smile returned, cold and triumphant. "Then we begin the ritual at dawn."

Back in the Citadel's archives, Orion and Lyra continued their search, their hands moving swiftly through the ancient texts. Lyra's eyes lit up as she found another piece of parchment, this one marked with a detailed account of the fireflies' connection to the Lightbringer.

"It says here that the fireflies can open the gateway between realms," she said, her voice hushed. "But only if the balance between light and shadow is maintained. If the balance is disrupted, it will lead to chaos—"

Orion's face paled. "The Shattered Veil."

Lyra's eyes widened in understanding. "If Cassian is being used to open it, and the balance isn't maintained—"

"He could unleash the darkness that's been sealed away for generations," Orion finished. "We have to find him before dawn."

They exchanged a look of determination, and Lyra tucked the parchments into her bag. "Let's go."

As they ascended the staircase, the fireflies hovered around them, their light guiding their way. The air was heavy with urgency, and Lyra felt the weight of what lay ahead. They had to find Cassian and stop the rogue magician's plan—before the fireflies' light was twisted into a force that could tear their world apart.

Chapter 8: The Lost Ritual

The first light of dawn broke over the horizon as Orion and Lyra emerged from the Citadel, their breath visible in the crisp morning air. The fireflies, sensing the urgency in their movements, swarmed around them, their glow illuminating the path through the forest. The siblings moved swiftly, guided by the map they had discovered in the archives, its lines marked with ancient runes that matched the patterns the fireflies had formed.

"We're running out of time," Orion said, his voice tense. "If they start the ritual before we get there, we might not be able to stop it."

Lyra's grip tightened on her flute. "We will. Cassian is still our brother. He will listen to us." She tried to ignore the doubt creeping into her voice, the fear that the rogue magician's influence might have taken hold of Cassian's heart. As they pushed through the undergrowth, the trees loomed like towering sentinels, and the shadows grew longer, stretching across their path.

The map led them to a clearing shrouded in mist, its center marked by a circle of stones carved with the same runes they had seen in the archives. At the heart of the circle stood an ancient altar, its surface covered in moss and etched with the symbols of the fireflies. Cassian and the rogue magician were already there, the fireflies clustering around them, their light flickering in anticipation.

"Cassian!" Lyra called out, her voice echoing through the clearing. Cassian turned, his eyes glowing with a strange intensity. For a moment, he looked like the brother she had always known—fierce, determined, and loyal. But then, as the rogue magician placed a hand on his shoulder, his expression hardened.

"Orion, Lyra," Cassian said, his voice steady. "I knew you had come. But you have to understand—I am doing this for all of us. The council has lied to us, and I will not let them control me any longer."

Orion stepped forward, his eyes locked on his brother. "Cassian, whatever they told you, it is not worth risking everything. The Lightbringer ritual—if it has done wrong, it could destroy everything our mother worked for."

The rogue magician's smile was cold as he watched the exchange. "And if it's done right, it will unlock the fireflies' true power—power that your mother was too afraid to wield."

Lyra's eyes pleaded with Cassian. "Please, listen to us. The fireflies are meant to maintain balance. If you use their power for anything else, you could unleash a darkness that none of us can control."

Cassian hesitated, his gaze shifting between his siblings and the rogue magician. For a brief moment, doubt flickered in his eyes. "I do not want to hurt anyone. I just want to know the truth."

The rogue magician's voice was smooth, filled with false promises. "The truth lies within the ritual, Cassian. The fireflies have chosen you—only through you can their light be fully realized."

Orion's hand went to the hilt of his blade, but Lyra raised her hand, signaling him to stop. She stepped closer, her eyes locked on Cassian's. "We can find the truth together, without risking everything. Do not let him manipulate you."

Cassian's face contorted with conflict, and he took a step back, the fireflies swirling around him as they pulsed with light. "You do not understand. I have seen what they can do. They can change everything."

Lyra's voice softened, her heart aching. "I know you want to honor Mother's legacy. But her legacy was not just about power. It was about protecting the balance, about keeping our world safe."

Cassian's eyes flicked to the rogue magician, who watched with cold detachment. "And if I walk away now? What then?"

The magician's smile vanished. "Then you remain in the shadows of your family's fear—trapped, like your mother before you." He raised his hands, and the fireflies' light intensified, casting long shadows over the clearing. The runes on the stones glowed, and the air filled with the hum of ancient magic.

Cassian's fists clenched as he felt the pull of the fireflies, their energy surging through him. His eyes met Lyra's, and for a moment, everything seemed to hang in the balance. Then, with a determined look, he stepped forward, placing his hand on the altar.

Orion's voice rang out, desperate. "Cassian, no!"

But it was too late. The fireflies erupted in a blinding flash of light, and the runes flared, their glow spreading across the stones. The air rippled as the magic of the ritual activated, pulling at the fabric of reality itself. The ground shook, and the sky above split open, revealing the swirling darkness of the Shattered Veil.

Lyra raised her flute, her fingers moving frantically as she played a melody that echoed through the clearing. The fireflies hesitated, their lights flickering as they responded to her music. She poured all her energy into the song, trying to guide them back, to break the spell that held them captive.

Cassian's face twisted with pain as he struggled to control the power coursing through him. "I can't... it's too strong..."

The rogue magician's eyes flashed with triumph. "Embrace it, Cassian. Let the fireflies' light guide you."

Orion charged forward, his blade drawn as he reached for Cassian. "You are stronger than this! Fight it!"

The fireflies swarmed around them, their light a blinding tempest as the magic of the ritual clashed with Lyra's melody. The clearing filled with the sound of her flute, the hum of the fireflies, and the roar of the Veil as it threatened to break open.

Cassian's hand trembled as he fought to pull away from the altar. "I cannot... I cannot do it alone..."

Lyra's music swelled, a song of hope and unity that resonated with the fireflies. She stepped closer, her eyes locked on Cassian's. "You are not alone. We are here."

Orion's hand reached out, gripping Cassian's arm. "Together, we can stop this."

Cassian's eyes met his brother's, and the determination in Orion's gaze anchored him. With a final surge of effort, he pulled his hand away from the altar, the connection breaking as the fireflies' light dimmed.

The rogue magician's face twisted in fury. "You fools! You have doomed us all!"

Orion and Cassian pulled back, and Lyra's music shifted, guiding the fireflies to seal the runes and close the rift in the sky. The darkness of the Veil receded, the clearing falling silent as the last echoes of the ritual faded.

The fireflies hovered, their light soft and gentle once more. Cassian fell to his knees, his breath ragged as he stared at his hands. "I am sorry... I did not know..."

Lyra knelt beside him, her eyes filled with relief. "It is okay. You are with us now."

Orion sheathed his blade, his expression softening as he looked down at his brother. "We will face whatever comes next together. That is what family does."

The rogue magician vanished into the shadows, his voice a whisper that lingered on the wind. "This is not over. The fireflies will choose their path, and when they do, you will see what you have sacrificed."

As the light of dawn bathed the clearing, the siblings stood together, their bond stronger than ever. The fireflies danced around them, their light a reminder of the balance they had sworn to protect. And though they knew the challenges were far from over, they faced the future with a newfound resolve—united, as their mother had always intended.

Chapter 9: The Crossroads

The dawn light filtered through the trees as the siblings returned to the Citadel, their faces marked with exhaustion and relief. The fireflies followed them, their glow gentle as they moved through the forest. Cassian walked between Orion and Lyra, his eyes downcast as the weight of his actions pressed on him. Lyra rested a hand on his shoulder, giving him a reassuring squeeze, but a shadow of doubt lingered in her eyes.

As they approached the gates, the fireflies' glow intensified, their light pulsing in urgent patterns. Orion stopped, his gaze shifting to the clusters of fireflies that hovered above. "They're trying to tell us something," he murmured.

Cassian looked up, his expression wary. "After everything, I'm not sure I want to know." The memory of the ritual's power still haunted him, and the rogue magician's words echoed in his mind. *The fireflies have chosen you—only through you can their light be fully realized.*

Lyra watched the fireflies, her fingers moving absently over her flute. "They have been guiding us all along, Cassian. We just need to listen."

As the siblings stepped through the gates, the council awaited them in the central chamber, their expressions grim. Master Eryndor's gaze fell on Cassian, his eyes filled with a mix of disappointment and concern. "You've come back, but the threat remains."

Orion crossed his arms, his voice edged with frustration. "We stopped the ritual, but the rogue magician is not done. He is determined to unlock the fireflies' power."

Master Eryndor's expression darkened, and he exchanged a glance with the other elders. "It is not the rogue magician you face. He is merely a vessel—one for a force much older and more dangerous than any of you understand."

Cassian frowned. "What do you mean?"

Eryndor's voice lowered, and the room seemed to grow colder. "The magician has been taken over by the spirit of an ancient evil—a sorcerer named Tharion. He once sought to wield the fireflies' power to alter the balance between light and darkness and reshape the world according to his will. Your mother, Evelyn, and your father, Lucian, confronted him long ago. Tharion had taken control of Lucian's body and used him as a pawn, but Evelyn fought to free him, ultimately sealing Tharion's spirit."

Lyra's eyes widened, and she felt a chill run down her spine. "The same sorcerer who controlled Father?"

Eryndor nodded. "Tharion's power was never utterly destroyed. It was contained, bound within the essence of the fireflies themselves. But now, he has found a new vessel—a magician hungry for power and willing to become his pawn."

Cassian's fists clenched, anger and guilt warring in his expression. "So, everything he told me—about Mother, about the fireflies—it was all part of his plan?"

Master Eryndor's gaze softened. "Tharion is an expert in manipulation. He twists the truth to suit his needs, using those who seek power for his own gain. He preyed on your desire for freedom, Cassian, just as he once preyed on your father's strength."

Orion's eyes blazed with determination. "We need to stop him before he can complete his plan. If he is controlling the magician, he will keep pushing until he unlocks the full power of the fireflies."

Lyra nodded, her voice firm. "And this time, he is using Cassian's connection to the fireflies as a weapon. If we are going to stop him, we need to find a way to sever that link."

Eryndor's expression became solemn. "There is one more thing. Evelyn once spoke of a guardian among the fireflies—a spirit named Eldrin. He is ancient and wise, a protector of their light. If you seek him out, he may offer guidance that no one else can. Find him, and perhaps he can help you break Tharion's hold."

Cassian's eyes met his sister's, and he felt a pang of regret. "I will do whatever it takes. I will not let him use me like he used Father."

Orion's face was set with resolve. "We find Eldrin first, and then we confront Tharion. Together."

The fireflies gathered around the siblings, their light forming a path that led deeper into the forest. Cassian felt their energy pulsing through him, and for the first time, he felt a sense of purpose—a chance to make things right. As they left the Citadel, he cast one last look at the council, a silent promise that he would not repeat the mistakes of the past.

The journey through the forest was long and filled with silence. The trees grew denser as they traveled, their ancient branches forming a canopy that blocked out the sky. The fireflies illuminated the way, their light flickering as they passed through shadows and tangled roots.

As they approached the Heart of the Glade, the air grew heavy with magic, and the fireflies' light brightened, revealing a hidden grove surrounded by massive stones inscribed with runes. At the center stood a pedestal, and atop it rested a small, glowing crystal—Evelyn's relic. But there was no sign of Eldrin.

Cassian stepped forward, his heart pounding. "This is it—the relic that can stop Tharion. But where is Eldrin?"

Orion nodded, his hand resting on the hilt of his blade. "We may need to perform the summoning chant. If Eldrin's spirit is nearby, the fireflies will respond."

Lyra raised her flute and played a soft, melodic tune that echoed through the grove. The fireflies began to circle, their light intensifying as they formed intricate patterns in the air. Cassian felt the magic around him shift, and the air grew warm.

But before they could complete the summoning, a chilly wind swept through the grove, and the shadows twisted, forming the figure of the rogue magician. His eyes burned with a sinister light, and his voice echoed, filled with a darkness that was not his own. "Foolish children. You think you can summon Eldrin and undo what I have set in motion?"

Lyra's flute was in her hands in an instant, and she played a quick, sharp melody. The fireflies responded, their light intensifying as they surrounded the magician. But the shadows only grew, and the air filled with the chilling laughter of Tharion.

"Your mother's sacrifice was for nothing," he taunted. "I have returned, and this time, I will not be stopped."

Cassian felt the pull of Tharion's magic, the temptation to surrender and let the darkness take him. But he remembered the look in Lyra's eyes, the determination in Orion's face, and he held firm. "You won't control me," he shouted. "I'm not your pawn!"

Orion raised his blade, and the fireflies formed a barrier of light around the siblings, pushing back the shadows. Lyra's music filled the air, weaving a melody of hope and unity that resonated with the fireflies' glow. The crystal pulsed in Cassian's hand, its light merging with the fireflies' power.

"Together," Orion said, his voice steady. "We end this."

Cassian raised the crystal, and Lyra's music surged, the fireflies swirling in a brilliant display of light. The shadows recoiled, and Tharion's voice shrieked with fury. "You cannot defeat me! I am eternal!"

But as Cassian placed the crystal on the pedestal, the light intensified, and the runes on the stones glowed, sealing the power within the grove. The shadows dissolved, and the rogue magician's form wavered, the darkness leaving his eyes as Tharion's presence was torn away.

With a final cry, the sorcerer's spirit was banished, the energy of the fireflies restoring the balance. The forest fell silent, the light of the crystal fading as the relic completed its work. Yet, in the silence, a single firefly hovered above them, its light bright and pure.

Cassian reached out, and the firefly landed gently on his hand. He knew in that moment—it was Eldrin. The ancient spirit had come to them, and he felt the firefly's energy flow through him, a sense of peace and clarity he had never known before.

Lyra knelt beside him, relief in her eyes. "We did it. Tharion is gone. And Eldrin... he is with us."

Orion extended a hand, pulling Cassian to his feet. "This is just the beginning. We still have a lot to do to restore the fireflies' balance, but with Eldrin's guidance, we will succeed."

Cassian nodded, a renewed determination in his eyes. "We will do it. Together."

As the fireflies danced around them, the siblings knew that their journey was far from over. But for the first time, they faced the future united, ready to honor their parents' legacy, protect the world they fought so hard to save, and follow Eldrin's guidance.

Chapter 10: Eldrin's Wisdom

The fireflies danced around the siblings as they stood in the grove, their glow gentle and warm. Cassian watched as the single firefly, Eldrin, hovered near his hand, its light bright and steady. There was something ancient and knowing in the way it moved, a presence that filled the grove with a sense of peace and clarity.

Orion and Lyra stood close, their eyes fixed on the small creature that now held their attention. "Eldrin..." Lyra whispered, her voice filled with wonder. "The guardian of the fireflies."

Orion nodded, his expression serious. "We have found him, but what now? The council said he would offer guidance. We need to know how to stop Tharion for good."

The firefly circled them, its light intensifying as it moved. Cassian felt its energy flow through him, a warmth that seemed to pierce the darkness that had lingered since the rogue magician's influence. "He's trying to communicate," Cassian said, his voice soft. "I can feel it."

Lyra raised her flute and played a soft melody, one that resonated with the fireflies' light. Eldrin's glow pulsed, and the air around them shimmered as the grove's magic responded. The runes on the stones brightened, casting intricate patterns of light across the ground.

Orion watched, his eyes narrowing as the light formed a path leading deeper into the forest. "He's showing us the way."

Cassian's gaze followed the trail of light, his heart pounding. "It must lead to something important—maybe another part of Mother's legacy."

The siblings exchanged a determined look before following the path Eldrin illuminated. The forest grew denser as they traveled, the air filled with the hum of magic as the fireflies guided them. The shadows stretched long beneath the trees, but with Eldrin's light, they felt a sense of protection and purpose.

As they walked, Cassian felt the weight of his mistakes lifting. For the first time, he believed they had a chance—not just to defeat Tharion but to honor their parents' legacy. "Mother always said the fireflies were more than just protectors," he said, his voice thoughtful. "I think she knew they were a bridge between light and darkness, and she believed in finding balance."

Lyra nodded, her eyes shining with hope. "Eldrin is proof of that. If he guided her, he could guide us."

Orion's hand rested on his blade as he scanned their surroundings, ever vigilant. "We will need every bit of guidance we can get. Tharion may be gone for now, but he will not stay banished forever. When he returns, he will be stronger."

Eldrin's light pulsed brighter as they reached the edge of a clearing. In the center stood a massive tree, its trunk twisted with age, and its branches reached high into the sky. The tree was unlike any they had seen before—its bark glowed faintly with the same energy as the fireflies, and its roots extended deep into the ground, covered in ancient runes.

Cassian felt a shiver run down his spine as he approached the tree. "This must be it—another part of Mother's legacy."

Lyra touched the tree's bark, her fingers tracing the runes. "It is connected to the fireflies. The energy feels... familiar."

Orion stepped forward, his gaze intent. "What does it mean?"

As if in response, Eldrin's light brightened, and the tree's runes glowed in unison. The air filled with a gentle hum, and the siblings felt the magic of the fireflies surge through them. In that moment, Cassian heard a voice—a whisper carried on the wind, ancient and wise.

"Seek the truth within the light," the voice said. "Only through unity and balance can you defeat the darkness."

Cassian's eyes widened. "Did you hear that?"

Lyra nodded, her eyes bright. "It is Eldrin. He is speaking to us."

Orion's expression softened, the weight of their mission settling in. "Mother's legacy wasn't just about sealing Tharion away—it was about ensuring that the balance between light and darkness remained, even after she was gone."

Eldrin circled the tree, his light illuminating the runes one by one. The siblings watched as a pattern emerged—a map etched into the tree's bark, showing paths that extended through the forest and beyond. Each path was marked with the symbols of the fireflies, indicating places of power.

Cassian traced the map with his fingers, his expression thoughtful. "These must be the places where the fireflies gather—points where their energy is strongest."

Lyra's eyes shone with understanding. "If we can connect these points, we can strengthen the fireflies' power and create a barrier strong enough to prevent Tharion from using their magic."

Orion's jaw clenched as he studied the map. "But if Tharion gets to these points first, he could corrupt them and twist the fireflies' power to his will."

Cassian met his brother's gaze, determination burning in his eyes. "Then we need to move fast. We have Eldrin's guidance, and we know what we have to do."

As the fireflies danced around them, the siblings felt a renewed sense of purpose. With Eldrin's light leading the way, they would journey to each point on the map, securing the fireflies' energy and ensuring that their power remained untainted. It was a race against time, and they knew that every step brought them closer to their final confrontation with Tharion.

Orion's hand rested on Cassian's shoulder. "We are doing this together. We will protect the fireflies and make sure Tharion never controls them again."

Lyra's flute echoed through the clearing, her melody blending with the fireflies' light. "For Mother, for Father, and for the balance they fought to protect."

Cassian nodded, feeling the warmth of their unity. "We'll honor their legacy."

With Eldrin lighting their path, the siblings turned to face the forest once more, ready to begin their journey to the points of power. As they walked, the fireflies formed a protective circle around them, their light a beacon of hope against the darkness that loomed on the horizon.

And so, the siblings set out, united in purpose, determined to protect the fireflies' magic and fulfill the mission their parents had entrusted to them. The path ahead was long, and the challenges were great, but with Eldrin's guidance and the bond they shared, they knew they had the strength to see it through.

Chapter 11: The First Point

The path through the forest seemed endless as the siblings journeyed to the first point of power marked on the map. Eldrin's light guided their way, the fireflies forming a trail that glowed softly against the darkening sky. The air was cool, and the whisper of the wind through the trees carried a sense of anticipation, as if the forest itself knew of the struggle ahead.

Cassian walked at the front, the map clutched in his hand. Every so often, he would glance down to check their progress, tracing the intricate patterns etched into the parchment. "We're getting close," he said, his voice steady. "The first point is just beyond the ridge."

Orion moved beside him, his hand resting on the hilt of his blade. "We need to be prepared. If Tharion knows we are moving to secure the fireflies' power, he might try to stop us."

Lyra, bringing up the rear, played a soft, calming melody on her flute. The fireflies responded, their light dancing to the rhythm of her song. "As long as we stay united, we'll succeed," she said, a hopeful note in her voice.

The forest thickened as they approached the ridge, the trees growing taller and the shadows deepening. The fireflies clustered around them, their glow illuminating the path. Cassian felt a sense of urgency as they pressed on, the weight of their mission heavy on his shoulders. "If we can secure this point, it will strengthen the fireflies' magic. It is the first step in protecting them from Tharion."

As they reached the top of the ridge, the landscape below opened up, revealing a vast clearing surrounded by towering ancient stones. At the center, a circle of fireflies hovered, their light bright and pulsating with energy. The air thrummed with magic, and Cassian knew they had found the first point.

Orion's eyes scanned the clearing, his expression wary. "It is quiet. Too quiet."

Lyra nodded, her fingers tightening around her flute. "Something doesn't feel right."

Eldrin hovered near Cassian, his light growing brighter as he circled above the stones. Cassian felt a warmth spread through him—a signal of reassurance. "We need to trust Eldrin. He is guiding us."

The siblings descended into the clearing, the fireflies forming a protective ring around them. As they approached the circle of stones, the ground beneath them trembled, and a chilly wind swept through the air. The shadows shifted, and Cassian's heart pounded as he saw figures emerging from the darkness—figures made of shadow and light, their eyes glowing with the same intensity as Tharion's.

Orion drew his blade, the steel glinting in the fireflies' glow. "Tharion's sent his minions to stop us."

Lyra raised her flute, and her music filled the clearing, a melody that resonated with the fireflies' light. The creatures hesitated, their forms flickering as the fireflies responded to her song. "We can weaken them if we work together," she said, her voice steady.

Cassian raised the crystal they had taken from the Heart of the Glade, its light merging with the fireflies' glow. "We protect the point and strengthen the fireflies' power. This is our fight."

The shadows lunged, and Orion met them with a swift strike, his blade cutting through the darkness. Cassian joined him, using the crystal's energy to repel the creatures, while Lyra's music wove through the air, keeping the fireflies' light strong. The siblings moved as one, their bond guiding their actions as they fought to secure the clearing.

The fireflies' light Intensified, and the ground beneath the stones glowed with ancient runes. Cassian felt the energy pulsing through him, and he knew they were close. "Lyra, play the summoning chant. We need Eldrin's power to seal this point."

Lyra's melody shifted, her song becoming a call to the ancient guardian. Eldrin's light flared, and the fireflies gathered in a tight formation, their glow merging with the runes. The shadows recoiled, their forms weakening as the fireflies' magic pushed them back.

Orion's blade flashed as he struck down the last of the creatures, and Cassian placed the crystal at the center of the stones. The runes glowed brighter, and the fireflies surrounded the crystal, their light filling the clearing.

"Now, Eldrin!" Cassian called, his voice echoing through the air.

Eldrin hovered above the crystal, his light merging with the fireflies' energy. The ground trembled, and the air hummed with magic as the power of the fireflies surged, creating a barrier that encircled the point. The shadows dissolved, and the clearing filled with a brilliant light as the runes sealed the magic within.

The siblings watched as the fireflies' glow settled, and the air grew still. Cassian felt the tension leave his body as he realized they had succeeded. "The point is secure."

Lyra lowered her flute, her eyes bright with relief. "We did it. Eldrin's guidance made it possible."

Orion sheathed his blade, his expression serious. "But this is just the beginning. We have more points to secure, and Tharion will not stop until he finds a way to break through."

Cassian nodded, his resolve strengthening. "We will move to the next point. With Eldrin's guidance, we will protect the fireflies and keep Tharion from corrupting their power."

As the siblings prepared to leave the clearing, Eldrin's light pulsed, and Cassian felt a gentle nudge in his mind—a message from the ancient guardian. "He's telling us there's a greater challenge ahead," Cassian said, his voice quietly. "Something more powerful than the shadows we faced here."

Orion's eyes met his, a hint of concern in his gaze. "We need to be ready for anything. Tharion will become more desperate as we strengthen the fireflies' power."

Lyra's melody shifted to a softer tune, and the fireflies formed a protective circle around the siblings as they left the clearing. The path ahead was uncertain, but with Eldrin's light guiding them, they felt a renewed sense of hope. The battle was far from over, but they were determined to see their mission through—to honor their parents' legacy and protect the balance of light and darkness that the fireflies maintained.

As they walked, the forest opened up before them, and the fireflies' glow lit their way. They were no longer alone in their fight—Eldrin's wisdom and the strength they found in each other would guide them through the trials ahead. Together, they would ensure that the fireflies' magic remained a force of balance and light.

Chapter 11: The First Point

The path through the forest seemed endless as the siblings journeyed to the first point of power marked on the map. Eldrin's light guided their way, the fireflies forming a trail that glowed softly against the darkening sky. The air was cool, and the whisper of the wind through the trees carried a sense of anticipation, as if the forest itself knew of the struggle ahead.

Cassian walked at the front, the map clutched in his hand. Every so often, he would glance down to check their progress, tracing the intricate patterns etched into the parchment. "We're getting close," he said, his voice steady. "The first point is just beyond the ridge."

Orion moved beside him, his hand resting on the hilt of his blade. "We need to be prepared. If Tharion knows we are moving to secure the fireflies' power, he might try to stop us."

Lyra, bringing up the rear, played a soft, calming melody on her flute. The fireflies responded, their light dancing to the rhythm of her song. "As long as we stay united, we'll succeed," she said, a hopeful note in her voice.

The forest thickened as they approached the ridge, the trees growing taller and the shadows deepening. The fireflies clustered around them, their glow illuminating the path. Cassian felt a sense of urgency as they pressed on, the weight of their mission heavy on his shoulders. "If we can secure this point, it will strengthen the fireflies' magic. It is the first step in protecting them from Tharion."

As they reached the top of the ridge, the landscape below opened up, revealing a vast clearing surrounded by towering ancient stones. At the center, a circle of fireflies hovered, their light bright and pulsating with energy. The air thrummed with magic, and Cassian knew they had found the first point.

Orion's eyes scanned the clearing, his expression wary. "It is quiet. Too quiet."

Lyra nodded, her fingers tightening around her flute. "Something doesn't feel right."

Eldrin hovered near Cassian, his light growing brighter as he circled above the stones. Cassian felt a warmth spread through him—a signal of reassurance. "We need to trust Eldrin. He is guiding us."

The siblings descended into the clearing, the fireflies forming a protective ring around them. As they approached the circle of stones, the ground beneath them trembled, and a chilly wind swept through the air. The shadows shifted, and Cassian's heart pounded as he saw figures emerging from the darkness—figures made of shadow and light, their eyes glowing with the same intensity as Tharion's.

Orion drew his blade, the steel glinting in the fireflies' glow. "Tharion's sent his minions to stop us."

Lyra raised her flute, and her music filled the clearing, a melody that resonated with the fireflies' light. The creatures hesitated, their forms flickering as the fireflies responded to her song. "We can weaken them if we work together," she said, her voice steady.

Cassian raised the crystal they had taken from the Heart of the Glade, its light merging with the fireflies' glow. "We protect the point and strengthen the fireflies' power. This is our fight."

The shadows lunged, and Orion met them with a swift strike, his blade cutting through the darkness. Cassian joined him, using the crystal's energy to repel the creatures, while Lyra's music wove through the air, keeping the fireflies' light strong. The siblings moved as one, their bond guiding their actions as they fought to secure the clearing.

The fireflies' light Intensified, and the ground beneath the stones glowed with ancient runes. Cassian felt the energy pulsing through him, and he knew they were close. "Lyra, play the summoning chant. We need Eldrin's power to seal this point."

Lyra's melody shifted, her song becoming a call to the ancient guardian. Eldrin's light flared, and the fireflies gathered in a tight formation, their glow merging with the runes. The shadows recoiled, their forms weakening as the fireflies' magic pushed them back.

Orion's blade flashed as he struck down the last of the creatures, and Cassian placed the crystal at the center of the stones. The runes glowed brighter, and the fireflies surrounded the crystal, their light filling the clearing.

"Now, Eldrin!" Cassian called, his voice echoing through the air.

Eldrin hovered above the crystal, his light merging with the fireflies' energy. The ground trembled, and the air hummed with magic as the power of the fireflies surged, creating a barrier that encircled the point. The shadows dissolved, and the clearing filled with a brilliant light as the runes sealed the magic within.

The siblings watched as the fireflies' glow settled, and the air grew still. Cassian felt the tension leave his body as he realized they had succeeded. "The point is secure."

Lyra lowered her flute, her eyes bright with relief. "We did it. Eldrin's guidance made it possible."

Orion sheathed his blade, his expression serious. "But this is just the beginning. We have more points to secure, and Tharion will not stop until he finds a way to break through."

Cassian nodded, his resolve strengthening. "We will move to the next point. With Eldrin's guidance, we will protect the fireflies and keep Tharion from corrupting their power."

As the siblings prepared to leave the clearing, Eldrin's light pulsed, and Cassian felt a gentle nudge in his mind—a message from the ancient guardian. "He's telling us there's a greater challenge ahead," Cassian said, his voice quietly. "Something more powerful than the shadows we faced here."

Orion's eyes met his, a hint of concern in his gaze. "We need to be ready for anything. Tharion will become more desperate as we strengthen the fireflies' power."

Lyra's melody shifted to a softer tune, and the fireflies formed a protective circle around the siblings as they left the clearing. The path ahead was uncertain, but with Eldrin's light guiding them, they felt a renewed sense of hope. The battle was far from over, but they were determined to see their mission through—to honor their parents' legacy and protect the balance of light and darkness that the fireflies maintained.

As they walked, the forest opened up before them, and the fireflies' glow lit their way. They were no longer alone in their fight—Eldrin's wisdom and the strength they found in each other would guide them through the trials ahead. Together, they would ensure that the fireflies' magic remained a force of balance and light.

Chapter 12: The Path of Shadows

The forest loomed ahead, its canopy thick and twisted, blocking out the sun's warmth. The fireflies' glow, which usually felt like a beacon of hope, seemed dimmer here, struggling to pierce through the shadows that clung to the trees. Cassian, Orion, and Lyra moved in silence, their footsteps muffled by the mossy ground. The air was cool, and a sense of foreboding hung over them, heavy like a shroud.

Eldrin hovered close to Cassian, his light steady but flickering occasionally, as if sensing the growing danger. Cassian glanced at the firefly guardian, his mind filled with the weight of their mission. "The path is narrowing," he said, checking the map he held. The runes on the parchment glowed faintly, guiding them forward. "The next point is just beyond that ridge."

Orion led the way, his grip firm on the hilt of his blade. "We should be ready for anything," he said, his voice low. "If Tharion knows we're moving to secure the points, he'll send his minions to stop us."

Lyra stayed close behind, her flute clutched in her hand. She had not played since they left the previous point, and the silence felt oppressive. "The closer we get to restoring the fireflies' power, the more Tharion's darkness will push back. We have to trust Eldrin."

Cassian nodded, but he felt a pang of doubt. He had always believed in the fireflies, in their ability to protect and guide, but after facing Tharion's power and seeing how easily he could corrupt that magic, a part of him wondered if they were truly prepared for what lay ahead. "Mother faced this same darkness," he murmured, more to himself than the others. "She must have felt the same fear."

Lyra looked over at him, her eyes soft with understanding. "And she pushed through it, Cassian. She believed in the balance she fought to protect." Her voice was filled with conviction, and it brought a flicker of hope to his heart.

The ridge they approached was steep, the rocks jagged and covered in vines. Cassian could feel the fireflies' energy growing stronger, pulsing in time with his heartbeat. He exchanged a glance with Orion, who nodded silently. They climbed the ridge, each step taking them closer to the glade where the next point of power awaited.

When they reached the top, the forest opened into a wide clearing surrounded by towering cliffs. The center was dominated by a massive stone pillar, its surface covered in runes that glowed faintly in the dim light. Fireflies hovered around it, their glow forming intricate patterns that moved like a dance, their magic alive and pulsating.

Cassian felt a chill run down his spine as he surveyed the scene. The energy here was different—more charged, more intense. "This is it," he said quietly. "The second point."

Orion's eyes scanned the cliffs, his expression wary. "It's too quiet."

Lyra's grip tightened on her flute, and her gaze darted to the shadows at the base of the cliffs. "Something is not right. I can feel it."

As if in response to her words, the shadows began to shift and writhe, spilling out from the crevices in the rock like smoke. Figures formed, their bodies insubstantial but menacing, their eyes glowing with the same eerie light they had seen in the rogue magician's eyes when Tharion controlled him. Cassian felt the darkness pressing in, its cold tendrils wrapping around his heart, urging him to doubt, to fear.

Orion drew his blade, the metal catching the light from the fireflies. "We knew this would not be easy. Lyra, we will need your music to keep the fireflies' light strong."

Lyra nodded, raising her flute. Her hands trembled for a moment, but she steadied herself and played a soft melody. The notes filled the clearing, echoing off the cliffs and weaving through the air. The fireflies responded, their glow brightening as they circled the siblings, forming a protective barrier.

Cassian watched as the shadows advanced, their forms becoming more defined, more real. He felt the familiar pull of fear, the whisper of doubt in his mind. What if we fail? What if Tharion is too strong for us? He gripped the crystal tighter, feeling its warmth flow into him, reminding him of his mother's courage. "We have to reach the pillar and activate the runes," he said, his voice firm. "It's the only way to secure this point."

Orion moved with purpose, his blade flashing as he met the shadows head-on. "Stay close, Cassian. We will make it."

Cassian joined his brother, holding the crystal aloft. Its light merged with the fireflies' glow, pushing back the darkness as they fought their way to the pillar. The shadows hissed, their forms twisting and recoiling, but for everyone they struck down, another seemed to rise, more powerful and determined.

Lyra's music shifted, becoming a song of strength and hope. She poured her energy into the melody, and the fireflies rallied, their light growing brighter, pushing against the encroaching darkness. "Eldrin, we need your power!" she called out, her voice steady despite the fear in her eyes.

Eldrin's light flared, and Cassian felt a surge of warmth as the ancient guardian moved to the pillar. The firefly's glow traced the runes etched into the stone, illuminating the patterns one by one. Cassian reached the base of the pillar and placed the crystal onto the runes. The energy flowed through him, and he felt a connection to the fireflies like never before—a bond that transcended time and space.

The shadows pushed harder, and the air grew colder as Tharion's power seeped into the clearing. Cassian could feel it—the pull of darkness, the whisper of surrender. "He's trying to break us," he said through gritted teeth. "We have to hold on."

Orion's blade clashed with the shadows, and he fought with a fierce determination. "Lyra, keep playing. Cassian, focus on the pillar."

Lyra's music swelled, a melody of defiance that filled the air with light. The fireflies responded, their energy merging with the crystal's glow. Cassian felt the power building, the fireflies' magic aligning with the runes. "We're almost there," he shouted. "Eldrin, now!"

Eldrin hovered above the crystal, his light merging with the fireflies' energy. The runes glowed brighter, and the ground trembled as the fireflies' power surged, creating a barrier that pulsed through the clearing. The shadows shrieked, their forms dissolving in the light.

The glade filled with a brilliant glow, the fireflies' energy sealing the power within the pillar. The shadows vanished, leaving the clearing bathed in the warm light of the fireflies. Cassian felt the tension leave his body as the magic stabilized. "We did it," he said, his voice filled with relief. "The point is secure."

Lyra lowered her flute, a tired but triumphant smile on her face. "Eldrin's guidance is working. We are protecting the fireflies, just like Mother did."

Orion sheathed his blade, his eyes scanning the cliffs. "But Tharion is becoming more desperate. Every point we secure strengthens us, but it also pushes him to fight harder."

Cassian looked at his siblings, his determination renewed. "We have to keep moving. We cannot let him get to the next point before us."

As they prepared to leave the glade, Eldrin's light flickered, and Cassian felt a wave of emotion—hope, fear, and a sense of warning. "He's telling us that Tharion is preparing something bigger," he said, his voice quiet. "Something beyond the shadows we've faced."

Orion's eyes darkened. "We need to stay vigilant. The closer we get to completing the map, the more he will fight to stop us."

Lyra played a soft, soothing melody as the fireflies formed a protective circle around them. The path ahead was uncertain, but with

Eldrin's guidance and the bond they shared, they felt a sense of purpose. The battles would grow harder, and Tharion's strength would only increase, but they knew they had the strength to see their mission through.

With the fireflies lighting their way, the siblings ventured deeper into the forest. Together, they moved forward, determined to honor their parents' legacy, and protect the balance of light and darkness.

Chapter 13: The Trials of the Glade

The forest felt alive with anticipation as the siblings made their way to the third point of power. The air was heavy, almost suffocating, and every shadow seemed to watch their movements. The fireflies' glow, though constant, seemed strained, flickering as if sensing the darkness that loomed closer with each step.

Eldrin hovered above, his light guiding them along the winding path. Cassian felt a mixture of fear and determination coursing through him. "The closer we get, the stronger Tharion's influence becomes," he said, his voice barely above a whisper.

Lyra played a soft, comforting tune on her flute, and the fireflies responded, their light brightening momentarily as if to push back the encroaching shadows. "We have to keep moving. The fireflies' magic depends on us."

Orion, ever vigilant, led the way, his blade at the ready. "The forest is changing," he noted, glancing around at the twisted trees and dense fog that began to rise from the ground. "It's like Tharion's presence is warping everything around us."

Cassian nodded, his hand resting on the map. The runes glowed faintly, leading them to the heart of the glade where the third point awaited. "Eldrin's light will guide us, but we need to be prepared for anything. Tharion knows what is at stake."

The path narrowed as they pressed forward, the trees closing in around them. The shadows lengthened, stretching like claws over the forest floor. Cassian could feel the magic in the air shifting, growing colder and darker. It reminded him of the stories his mother used to tell him, stories of how she and his father had fought to protect the fireflies' magic. "She faced this too," he said, trying to draw strength from the memory. "Mother fought the darkness, and so will we."

Lyra's eyes met his, a spark of determination in her gaze. "And she did it with Father by her side. We have each other, just like they did."

Orion's expression softened as he looked at his siblings. "We are stronger together. We have come this far because of the bond we share."

Eldrin pulsed brightly, his light forming a path that led through the thickening fog. The siblings followed their steps quietly and carefully. The air grew colder, and the fog seemed to swirl with whispers, voices that felt both familiar and foreign. Cassian felt a shiver run down his spine as the whispers grew louder, echoing in his mind.

"Do you hear that?" he asked, his voice tense.

Lyra nodded, her fingers tightening around her flute. "It's like they're calling to us, trying to pull us in."

Orion's grip on his blade tightened. "Stay focused. It is Tharion's influence. He is trying to distract us, to weaken our resolve."

The fog parted, revealing the entrance to the glade. The fireflies' light illuminated the way, casting long shadows over the stones that surrounded the clearing. At the center stood a large, ancient tree, its bark covered in glowing runes. The fireflies clustered around it, their light forming a protective barrier.

Cassian's eyes widened as he saw the tree's runes. "This is it—the third point." He could feel the magic emanating from the tree, a powerful energy that pulsed in rhythm with the fireflies' light. "We need to activate the runes to strengthen the barrier."

But as they stepped into the clearing, the ground beneath them shuddered, and the air grew colder. The shadows that clung to the edges of the glade began to move, taking shape and coalescing into dark figures. Their eyes glowed with the same malevolent light as Tharion's, and their forms twisted as they advanced.

Orion raised his blade, his stance shifting as he prepared for the fight. "Lyra, keep the fireflies' light strong. We cannot let them reach the tree."

Lyra lifted her flute and played a quick, sharp melody. The fireflies responded, their glow brightening as they formed a protective barrier around the tree. Cassian felt the energy of their unity, but he also felt the weight of the shadows pressing in, their whispers growing louder.

The figures lunged, and Orion met them with swift strikes, his blade slicing through the darkness. Cassian joined him, raising the crystal and channeling its energy into the fireflies. The crystal's light merged with the fireflies' glow, pushing back the shadows, but for every shadow they dispelled, more seemed to emerge from the darkness.

Lyra's music intensified, her melody weaving through the air, a song of strength and unity that filled the clearing. The fireflies surged, their light creating a barrier that held the shadows at bay, but the darkness pushed back, its power growing stronger. "Eldrin, guide us!" she called, her voice echoing through the glade.

Eldrin hovered above the tree, his light brightening as he traced the runes on its bark. Cassian felt a connection form—a bond that tied them all together, a link between the fireflies, Eldrin, and his own magic. "We have to activate the runes," he shouted. "It's the only way to seal this point."

He ran to the tree, placing his hand on the bark. The runes glowed under his touch, and he felt the magic flow through him, the fireflies' energy merging with his own. But the shadows surged, their whispers turning into shouts that filled his mind with doubt. You are not strong enough. You will fail like the others before you.

Cassian gritted his teeth, fighting against the fear. "We can do this," he said, his voice steady. "We have to trust each other."

Orion fought fiercely, his blade flashing as he defended the clearing. "We've come too far to turn back now," he said, his eyes fierce. "Lyra, keep playing."

Lyra's music swelled, her melody resonating with the fireflies' light. The tree's runes pulsed, and the fireflies gathered around Cassian, their energy flowing into the crystal he held. "We're almost there, Cassian!" she shouted, her voice filled with hope.

Eldrin's light flared, and the runes on the tree glowed brighter. Cassian felt the connection deepen, the fireflies' energy merging with his own as he channeled it into the tree. The ground trembled, and the air filled with the hum of magic as the fireflies' power surged, pushing back the darkness.

But the shadows fought harder, their forms growing stronger as they tried to breach the barrier. Cassian felt the pressure building, the weight of their whispers clawing in his mind. "We have to hold on," he said through gritted teeth. "Eldrin, now!"

Eldrin circled above, his light merging with the fireflies.' The tree's runes pulsed one last time, and the energy exploded outward, filling the clearing with a blinding light. The shadows shrieked as the magic of the fireflies sealed the point, dissolving their forms and banishing the darkness.

The glade fell silent, the fireflies' glow softening as the runes stabilized. Cassian stepped back, breathing heavily as he felt the tension leave his body. "We did it," he said, relief washing over him. "The point is secure."

Lyra lowered her flute, her eyes bright with triumph. "Eldrin's guidance made it possible. We are protecting the fireflies, just like Mother did."

Orion sheathed his blade, his expression still tense. "But Tharion's influence is growing stronger. Every point we secure only makes him more desperate."

Cassian met his siblings' gaze, determination etched on his face. "Then we move to the next point. We cannot let him corrupt the fireflies' magic."

As they prepared to leave, Eldrin's light flickered, and Cassian felt a wave of emotion—a warning of something greater yet to come. "He's telling us there's a final trial ahead," Cassian said, his voice quietly. "Something beyond anything we've faced so far."

Orion's eyes darkened. "We need to stay vigilant. The closer we get to securing all the points, the harder Tharion will fight to stop us."

Lyra played a soft, soothing melody as the fireflies formed a protective circle around the siblings. The forest stretched before them, the path uncertain, but with Eldrin's guidance and their bond, they felt a sense of hope. They knew the battles would grow harder, and Tharion's strength would only increase, but they were ready.

The fireflies lit their path as they ventured deeper into the forest. Together, they walked forward, united in purpose and determined to protect the balance of light and darkness.

Chapter 14: The Echoes of Doubt

The forest felt more oppressive as the siblings pressed onward. The canopy overhead blocked out the sun, leaving them bathed only in the faint glow of the fireflies. The trees loomed tall and twisted, their branches reaching out like claws. Shadows danced along the path, shifting in ways that made Cassian feel like they were being watched from all sides.

Eldrin's light was their only guide, and even it flickered now, as if the ancient guardian sensed the growing darkness. The air was thick with magic—both the familiar warmth of the fireflies and the cold, invasive energy that Cassian knew was Tharion's. "The path ahead is changing," he said, his voice hushed. "The map shows the fourth point is near, but it feels like everything around us is... bending."

Orion's eyes narrowed as he scanned the path. "Tharion's power is warping the forest. He knows we are close." His hand rested on the hilt of his blade, the tension in his shoulders clear. "We have to stay together."

Lyra nodded, but Cassian saw the uncertainty in her eyes. "Every step we take, it feels like we're moving deeper into his grasp." She gripped her flute tightly, the familiar weight of it grounding her. "Eldrin is trying to guide us, but Tharion is pulling us in another direction."

Cassian exchanged a glance with Orion. "We trust Eldrin. Mother believed in him, and he has been guiding us this far." He tried to sound confident, but deep down, a knot of worry tightened in his chest. The forest felt like it was closing in around them, and each step felt heavier, as if they were wading through darkness itself.

The path opened into another clearing, but unlike the others they had seen, this one was surrounded by mirrors—large, ancient structures reflecting twisted, distorted images of the forest. The fireflies hovered above, their light struggling to illuminate the space. At the center of the clearing stood an obelisk, its surface covered in runes that glowed faintly. The fireflies clustered around it, their light forming a protective barrier.

Cassian felt a chill run down his spine as he looked at the mirrors. They reflected not just the forest but also himself, Lyra, and Orion—only their reflections were different. Darker. Their eyes were shadowed, and their expressions twisted with doubt and fear. "This isn't right," he muttered. "It's some kind of illusion."

Orion gripped his blade, his eyes darting between the mirrors. "It is Tharion's doing. He is using these reflections to manipulate us, to weaken our resolve."

Lyra raised her flute, her eyes filled with determination. "We need to break the illusion. If we can reach the obelisk, we can activate the runes and secure the point."

But as she lifted the flute to her lips, the mirrors flickered, and the reflections changed. Cassian saw himself, but it was a version filled with anger and darkness. The reflection spoke, its voice echoing through the clearing. "You will never be strong enough, Cassian. You have always been afraid—afraid of failing, afraid of being alone. You cannot protect anyone."

The words pierced him like a knife. Cassian felt the weight of his own doubts crashing over him. "It's not real," he whispered, but the fear gnawed at him. What if it is right? What if I am not strong enough?

Lyra's melody wavered, and her eyes widened as she saw her own reflection—one filled with sorrow. "You are just a shadow of what you could be, Lyra. Always following, never leading. You will lose everyone you care about."

Orion's reflection stepped out of the mirror, a sneer on its face. "You think you are a protector, Orion, but you cannot save anyone. You are just like Father, letting others pay the price for your mistakes."

The shadows in the clearing thickened, and the whispers from the mirrors grew louder, filling the air with accusations and fears. The fireflies' light flickered, and Cassian felt the ground beneath him tremble. "It's trying to tear us apart," he said, his voice tight with emotion. "We have to stay together."

Orion's grip on his blade faltered, his eyes locked on his own reflection. "I have always wondered... if I could have done more. If I could have been stronger for all of us." His voice was filled with doubt, and Cassian saw the pain in his brother's eyes.

Lyra's music softened, her hands trembling. "I'm afraid too," she admitted, her voice breaking. "Afraid of failing all of you."

Cassian felt his own fear clawing at him, but he knew that if they let the illusions take hold, they would be lost. He reached out, taking Lyra's hand, and then Orion's. "We cannot give in to this. Tharion wants to divide us, to use our fears against us." He tightened his grip, his eyes burning with determination. "But we are stronger than this. We are stronger together."

Eldrin's light flared, and the fireflies responded, their glow brightening as they surrounded the siblings. Cassian felt the warmth of their magic, a reminder of the bond they shared. "Mother believed in the fireflies. She believed in us."

Lyra's music grew stronger, the melody shifting into a song of unity and courage. The fireflies' light pulsed in rhythm with the music, pushing back the shadows. Cassian felt the energy flowing through him, and he knew they had to act now.

"Orion, we need to reach the obelisk and activate the runes," Cassian said, his voice steady. "Lyra, keep the fireflies' light strong."

Orion nodded, his grip on his blade tightening as he fought against the illusions. "Let's end this."

The siblings moved as one, their bond guiding them as they advanced toward the obelisk. The shadows lashed out, and the reflections in the mirrors screamed, but Cassian held firm, channeling the fireflies' energy through the crystal. "Eldrin, guide us!"

Eldrin's light brightened, tracing the runes on the obelisk. Cassian placed the crystal on its surface, feeling the magic flow through him. The fireflies clustered around the obelisk, their light merging with the runes as the energy surged.

Lyra's music filled the clearing, overpowering the whispers. The mirrors flickered, and the reflections wavered, their power weakening as the fireflies' light grew. "We're almost there!" Lyra called out, her eyes filled with determination.

Orion fought back the remaining shadows, his blade flashing as he defended the path to the obelisk. "Keep pushing, Cassian!"

Cassian felt the energy build, the fireflies' light merging with the crystal and the runes. The obelisk pulsed, and the ground beneath them shook as the magic of the fireflies sealed the point. The shadows screamed as they dissolved, and the mirrors shattered, their fragments falling to the ground like rain.

The clearing filled with light, and the fireflies' glow stabilized, sealing the magic within the obelisk. The darkness dissipated, leaving only the warmth of the fireflies' energy. Cassian stepped back, breathing heavily as relief washed over him. "We did it. The point is secure."

Lyra lowered her flute, her eyes bright with triumph but also lingering sadness. "Tharion's power is strong, but we're stronger."

Orion sheathed his blade, his expression thoughtful. "The illusions tried to use our fears against us, but we overcame them together."

Cassian met his siblings' gaze, gratitude and resolve filling his heart. "We have to keep trusting each other. We cannot let him divide us."

Eldrin hovered above them, his light soft and warm, a reminder of the unity they shared. Cassian felt the guardian's presence, a reassurance that they were on the right path. "Eldrin is with us. We will protect the fireflies, just like Mother did."

As they prepared to leave the glade, Cassian felt a wave of hope wash over him. The path ahead was uncertain, but with his siblings and Eldrin by his side, he knew they had the strength to face whatever challenges lay ahead. The fireflies' light guided them as they ventured deeper into the forest, united in their mission to protect the balance of light and darkness.

Chapter 15: The Final Point

The forest felt like a living entity, its branches curling like fingers reaching for the siblings as they moved through the dense undergrowth. The fireflies' light, which had guided them through the previous points, seemed weaker here, flickering as if struggling against an unseen force. The air was heavy, filled with an energy that crackled with tension and foreboding.

Cassian led the way, his eyes fixed on the map. The runes glowed faintly, and the lines that had once seemed clear now blurred as if the path itself was shifting. "The fifth point is close," he said, but his voice lacked Its usual confidence. "Tharion's influence is stronger here. We need to stay focused."

Orion walked beside him, his blade drawn. "He knows this is the decisive point. If we secure it, the fireflies' magic will be strong enough to counter his power. He will not let us take it easily."

Lyra moved cautiously behind them, her flute ready in her hand. "The fireflies are struggling against him. We will have to rely on our bond more than ever."

Eldrin hovered above them, his light pulsing with urgency. Cassian felt the ancient guardian's energy flow through him—a connection that had grown stronger with each point they secured. "Eldrin is telling us to hurry. Tharion is preparing something big."

As they pressed forward, the path opened into a clearing, but unlike the others, this one was barren. The trees around the edges twisted like gnarled claws, and the ground was covered in ash. In the center stood a massive stone archway, its surface etched with runes that glowed faintly in the dim light. Fireflies hovered around it, their light dim and flickering as they fought against the darkness that clung to the air.

"This is it," Cassian said, his voice filled with both determination and trepidation. "The final point."

Orion's eyes scanned the clearing, his grip tightening on his blade. "We will have to act fast. If Tharion's magic is strong enough to warp the fireflies' light, he is close."

Lyra lifted her flute, her eyes fixed on the archway. "We need to activate the runes and strengthen the fireflies' barrier. If we succeed, it will disrupt Tharion's control."

But as she raised her flute to play, the air around them grew colder, and a low, rumbling sound echoed through the clearing. The ground beneath them trembled, and Cassian felt the chill of Tharion's presence seep into his bones. "He's here," he whispered. "He's trying to stop us."

The shadows around the clearing shifted, and the archway's runes darkened, their glow flickering as if being drained of energy. Figures began to emerge from the darkness—creatures formed of shadow and fire, their eyes glowing with Tharion's power. They moved with an unnatural grace, their forms twisting and changing as they advanced.

Orion's blade flashed as he prepared for the fight. "Lyra, play. We will hold them off."

Lyra nodded, her hands steady as she began to play a melody that resonated through the clearing. The fireflies responded, their light brightening as they formed a protective circle around the siblings. Cassian raised the crystal, channeling its energy into the fireflies, but the darkness pushed back, its power clawing at their defenses.

The creatures lunged, and Orion met them head-on, his blade cutting through the shadows. Cassian felt the pressure building, the weight of Tharion's magic pressing down on them. "We have to reach the archway!" he shouted. "It's the only way to secure the point."

Orion's movements were quick and precise, but the creatures were relentless. For every shadow he struck down, another emerged, stronger than the last. "Go, Cassian!" he called, his voice strained. "I'll hold them off."

Cassian ran toward the archway, the crystal's light pulsing in his hand. The runes on the stone flickered as he approached, and the fireflies' light dimmed under the force of Tharion's power. He could feel the darkness creeping into his mind, whispering doubts and fears. You are too late. You cannot save them. You will only fail.

Lyra's music intensified, her melody shifting into a song of hope and unity. The fireflies rallied, their light brightening as they pushed against the darkness. "Cassian, focus!" she called, her voice carrying through the chaos. "Trust Eldrin!"

Eldrin's light flared, and Cassian felt the guardian's energy surge through him. He placed his hand on the archway's runes, feeling their power pulse beneath his fingers. "Eldrin, help us seal the point," he whispered, his voice filled with urgency.

The crystal merged with the runes, and the fireflies gathered around, their light forming a barrier. But the darkness fought back, and Cassian felt his strength waver. The whispers grew louder, and the shadows clawed at his mind. You will fail, just like before. You cannot protect anyone.

He closed his eyes, focusing on the connection he felt with Eldrin and his siblings. "We're stronger together," he said, his voice steady. "I trust you."

Orion's blade flashed as he fought back the creatures, his movements a blur of determination. "Lyra, keep playing!"

Lyra's melody swelled, her music blending with the fireflies' light. The runes on the archway pulsed, and Cassian felt the energy building, the power of the fireflies surging through him. "We're almost there!" he shouted, his eyes locked on the runes.

Eldrin hovered above the archway, his light merging with the fireflies.' The runes glowed brighter, and the ground beneath them shook as the magic of the fireflies filled the clearing. The shadows recoiled, their forms dissolving in the light.

But as the energy reached its peak, the air around them rippled, and a figure emerged from the darkness—a towering presence cloaked in shadow, his eyes burning with an ancient, malevolent power. Tharion.

Cassian felt the force of his presence, a wave of darkness that threatened to overwhelm him. "He's here!" he shouted, raising the crystal to shield himself.

Tharion's voice echoed through the clearing, a low, mocking whisper. "You think you can stop me, children of Evelyn? You are but shadows, playing at being heroes."

Orion stepped forward, his blade at the ready. "We won't let you take the fireflies' power."

Lyra's music filled the air, and the fireflies' light intensified, pushing back against Tharion's presence. Cassian felt their unity, the strength they shared. "We are not afraid of you," he said, his voice filled with determination. "We know the truth, and we won't be divided."

Tharion's form wavered, and he raised a hand, sending a wave of dark energy toward them. The fireflies surged, their light forming a barrier that absorbed the impact. Cassian channeled the crystal's energy into the archway, and the runes pulsed, sealing the point's power.

Eldrin's light flared, and the fireflies merged their energy, creating a brilliant glow that filled the clearing. Tharion's form flickered, and he hissed as the magic pushed him back. "This isn't over," he snarled. "You may have won this battle, but the war is far from finished."

With a final surge of energy, the shadows dissolved, and the clearing fell silent. The runes on the archway glowed steadily, and the fireflies' light stabilized, sealing the point's power.

Cassian collapsed to his knees, breathing heavily. "We did it... but he'll be back."

Lyra lowered her flute, her eyes filled with resolve. "We have to be ready. This was only the beginning."

Orion sheathed his blade, his expression serious. "The fireflies' power is strong, but we need to be stronger. We will prepare for the ultimate battle."

Eldrin hovered above them, his light a beacon of hope. Cassian felt the guardian's presence, a reminder that they were not alone. "We'll fight together," he said, looking at his siblings. "And we'll protect the fireflies, just like Mother did."

As they left the clearing, the fireflies formed a protective circle around them, their light guiding their path. The forest stretched before them, the path uncertain but filled with purpose. They knew the challenges would grow harder, but with Eldrin's guidance and their unity, they were ready to face whatever lay ahead.

Chapter 16: The Final Point

The path back to the Citadel felt heavier than before, weighed down by more than just exhaustion. The fireflies hovered close, their glow flickering in the dim light of dusk. Though they had secured the last point, the taste of victory was bittersweet. Tharion had shown himself, not just as a distant threat but as a real, powerful force that loomed closer than ever.

Cassian walked ahead, silent. The crystal felt heavier in his hands now, like it held the weight of his own doubts as much as the magic of the fireflies. We are not ready, he thought, though he kept the words to himself. He glanced over at Eldrin, whose light seemed more subdued, dimmer than it had been before. Even their ancient guardian felt the strain of what was to come.

Orion walked beside him, his eyes scanning the horizon, always watching, always ready. "We can't let him catch us off guard," he said, his voice rough, like he had been carrying the weight of a leader far too long. "Tharion will not wait for us to regroup. We need to be ready the moment we get back."

Lyra, trailing slightly behind, held her flute in both hands, her fingers tapping anxiously against it. "The fireflies... they have been quieter since we left the last point. They are holding something back. I can feel it." Her voice, usually filled with lightness and song, was tinged with a nervousness she tried to mask.

Cassian stopped for a moment, turning to face his siblings. "Do you think they are waiting for us? Or for Tharion?" His voice was quieter than usual, as though he were afraid to speak the answer aloud.

Lyra hesitated, her eyes drifting to the fireflies. "It is like they know something we do not. Almost like they are bracing themselves... for whatever comes next."

Orion tightened his grip on the hilt of his blade, the muscles in his jaw flexing. "Then we need to do the same."

As they approached the gates of the Citadel, the stone walls felt colder than before, as if the very structure sensed the tension building in the air. The council awaited them in the main hall, their faces shadowed with a mix of relief and worry. Master Eryndor stepped forward, his gaze sweeping over the siblings.

"You've done well," he said, though his tone carried the weight of what he would say next. "Securing the five points was crucial. But now... you must prepare for what is coming. Tharion will not wait long."

Cassian stepped forward, holding up the crystal. "We saw him at the last point. He was... different. Stronger. His power was overwhelming."

Master Eryndor nodded gravely. "He is growing desperate. And with desperation comes recklessness. You may be his final obstacle, but that also means you are his primary target."

Orion clenched his fist. "We know he is coming. But how do we stop him? We have only delayed him, not defeated him."

Eryndor studied Orion for a moment, then spoke slowly. "It is not just about defeating him, Orion. It is about outlasting him. Tharion's power thrives on fear and doubt. He uses them to weaken his enemies, just as he did to you at the last point. But you are stronger than that."

Lyra looked at the council, her voice hesitant but firm. "The fireflies have been holding something back. It is like they are waiting... for the right moment."

Eryndor's expression softened. "The fireflies have been preparing for this moment long before any of us were here. They know when the balance will shift, and they will release their full power when it is needed most. But you must be ready to guide that power."

Cassian met Eryndor's gaze, feeling the weight of his words. "How can we be ready for that? How can we be sure we will not fail?"

Eryndor's eyes held a quiet wisdom. "You will not face him alone. You have each other, and you have the fireflies. The key to defeating Tharion is not just strength—it is unity. The same bond that has carried you this far will carry you through the last battle."

Cassian glanced at his siblings, feeling a swell of emotion. They had faced so much together—doubt, fear, and danger—and through it all, they had only grown stronger. His fear of failing them gnawed at him, but Eryndor's words planted a seed of hope.

Lyra stepped forward, her eyes determined. "We will face him. And we will win. Not just for the fireflies, but for everything our mother fought for."

Orion nodded, his jaw set. "Whatever it takes."

Cassian looked down at the crystal in his hands, its glow steady and constant, like a heartbeat. He could feel the fireflies' energy, a reminder that they were not alone. "We'll be ready," he said, his voice firmer now. "We'll fight, together."

That night, the siblings sat in the Citadel courtyard, the fireflies hovering close, their light brighter now in the stillness of the night. Cassian sat with his back against the cool stone, the crystal resting in his lap, its light flickering softly. The stars above felt distant, and yet there was something comforting about their silent presence.

Lyra was sitting beside him, her flute in her lap, though she was not playing. She looked out at the fireflies, her face contemplative. "Do you ever wonder," she said quietly, "what Mother and Father felt when they faced Tharion? Did they know what it would cost them?"

Cassian's throat tightened at the mention of their parents. "I think they knew," he replied, his voice soft. "But they did not care about the cost. They just wanted to protect us... and the fireflies."

Orion stood a little way off, his gaze focused on the horizon. "We're not them," he said, though there was no bitterness in his voice. "But we are here because of them. And we will finish what they started."

Cassian felt a surge of emotion, his chest tightening with both pride and fear. "This fight... it is bigger than all of us. But it is also about us. About whom we are. About what we will leave behind."

Lyra smiled faintly. "And we will leave behind a world where the fireflies can keep the balance. Just like Mother wanted."

Eldrin hovered above them, his light steady and warm. Cassian could feel the ancient guardian's presence, a reminder that they were never truly alone. "We'll face Tharion together," he said quietly. "And we'll make sure he doesn't destroy what they sacrificed to protect."

The fireflies danced in the air around them, their light a soft glow that wrapped around the siblings like a protective shield. The night stretched on, but there was a sense of calm in the stillness, a brief moment of peace before the storm.

They were ready.

Chapter 17: The Final Convergence

The air in the Citadel was thick with an uneasy stillness. The fireflies hovered restlessly around the courtyard, their light pulsing in uneven patterns. The once-steady glow that had guided the siblings through every challenge now seemed unstable, flickering as if it were struggling to maintain its brightness. Even Eldrin, usually a constant presence of calm, shimmered in a way that made Cassian uneasy.

The three siblings stood in silence, looking out over the stone walls of the Citadel, where the forest beyond was cloaked in an unnatural darkness. Tharion's presence was everywhere now, pressing in from the edges of the world like a shadow creeping across the land.

Orion was the first to break the silence. His hand rested on the hilt of his sword, fingers tightening around the worn leather grip. "It's happening," he said, his voice low but resolute. "Tharion's power is growing. He is preparing to strike."

Cassian nodded, his eyes fixed on the horizon. The final confrontation was closer than ever, and the weight of that realization settled heavily on his shoulders. "We can feel him everywhere now. The fireflies are reacting to his presence." He held the crystal in his hands, feeling its faint pulse in rhythm with his own heartbeat.

Lyra stepped forward, her flute in hand. "They're afraid," she whispered, her voice barely audible. "The fireflies are afraid. I have never felt them like this before."

Orion's jaw clenched, and he scanned the tree line, watching as the shadows seemed to shift and move. "Fear is exactly what Tharion wants. He thrives on it. He is trying to break their resolve... and ours."

Cassian took a deep breath, feeling the cool air fill his lungs. He turned to face his siblings, his voice steady but filled with the weight of what was to come. "We need to be ready for him. Tharion will not stop until he is consumed everything—the fireflies, the magic, us."

Lyra's fingers tightened around her flute. "And if we cannot stop him? What if the fireflies cannot hold him back?"

Cassian met her gaze, his heart heavy with doubt, but he could not let it show. "We will not let that happen. We have come too far, and we have been through too much to let him win now."

As if in response to his words, Eldrin flickered brightly, his light pulsing with sudden urgency. Cassian looked up at the guardian, feeling a wave of energy pass through him—a signal. "Eldrin is telling us something. He is saying... it is time."

Orion straightened, his eyes narrowing as he looked at Cassian. "Time for what?"

Cassian closed his eyes, trying to connect with the ancient guardian's message. The fireflies' energy flowed through him, and in that moment, he understood. "It is time to meet him. Tharion will not wait any longer. We need to face him before he destroys everything."

Lyra's breath hitched, and she looked between her brothers, her face pale but determined. "Where?"

Cassian opened his eyes, the answer clear now. "At the Heart of the Glade. That is where this ends."

The journey to the Heart of the Glade was faster than it should have been, but the fireflies' light pulled them forward as if the very magic of the forest were guiding them. The trees bent and swayed unnaturally, and the air was thick with tension. Every shadow seemed to flicker with movement, and the ground beneath their feet trembled with a slow, ominous rhythm.

The Heart of the Glade was a place of ancient magic, a sacred site where the fireflies' power had once been the strongest. Now, it felt hollow, as if something had drained it of its life force. The runes on the ancient stones that encircled the glade flickered weakly, their once-brilliant light now dim and fading.

As the siblings stepped into the clearing, the air grew colder, and a sense of dread settled over them. Cassian held the crystal tightly, feeling its power resonate with the weakening energy around them. "He's here," he whispered, his voice barely audible.

The shadows at the far edge of the glade began to shift, and from the darkness, a figure emerged—tall, cloaked in shadow, his eyes glowing with a malevolent light. Tharion.

The ancient sorcerer's presence filled the clearing, a palpable force that pressed against them from all sides. His voice echoed through the air, low and filled with mocking amusement. "So, the children of Evelyn have come to face me at last. How... predictable."

Orion stepped forward, his blade gleaming in the dim light of the fireflies. "We are not afraid of you, Tharion. This ends now."

Tharion's laughter echoed through the glade, a sound that sent shivers down Cassian's spine. "Ends? Oh no, this is just the beginning. The fireflies' power will be mine, and there is nothing you can do to stop me."

Cassian felt the crystal in his hand pulse with energy, but it was faint, weaker than before. He glanced at his siblings, seeing the tension in their faces, the weight of the battle that was about to begin. "We'll stop you," he said, his voice steady despite the fear gnawing at him. "We'll protect the fireflies, just like our mother did."

Tharion's eyes burned with dark fire. "Your mother was a fool. She thought she could defeat me and look where that got her. Dead. Her sacrifice was meaningless."

Cassian's chest tightened, anger flaring inside him. "You are wrong. She did not fight alone, and neither will we."

Lyra raised her flute, and the soft, haunting melody filled the air, the fireflies responding to her call. Their light brightened, forming a circle around the siblings, a barrier of magic that pushed back against Tharion's dark presence.

Tharion sneered, his form shifting and growing darker. "Futile. Do you think your little tricks can stop me? I will consume you all, and the fireflies will be mine."

Orion moved closer to Cassian, his eyes sharp with determination. "We do this together."

Cassian nodded, his grip tightening on the crystal. "For Mother. For everything she fought for."

With a deafening roar, Tharion unleashed a wave of dark energy, and the battle began.

The ground shook beneath them as the force of Tharion's power collided with the fireflies' light. Cassian felt the crystal pulse in his hand, its energy flickering in time with the fireflies surrounding them. Lyra's melody intensified, her song weaving through the magic in the air, holding their protective barrier steady.

Orion charged forward, his blade flashing as he met Tharion's attack head-on. The dark energy swirled around him, but the fireflies' light pushed back, forming a shield that deflected the worst of the impact.

Cassian focused all his energy on the crystal, feeling its connection to the fireflies deepen. He could feel their fear, their desperation, but also their hope. They were waiting—for the moment when their full power would be released.

Lyra's song wavered as Tharion's dark magic pressed harder against their defenses, and Cassian's heart raced. "We need to end this now," he called out, his voice filled with urgency. "We can't hold him off for long."

Orion fought fiercely, his strikes precise and relentless, but Tharion's power was overwhelming, and with every blow Orion landed, the sorcerer grew stronger. "Cassian!" he shouted, his voice strained. "Whatever you're going to do, do it now!"

Cassian felt the fireflies' energy surge through him, a sudden wave of strength that filled him with certainty. "It's time," he whispered, his eyes locking on Tharion's dark form.

He raised the crystal and Eldrin flared brightly above them, the ancient guardian's light merging with the fireflies.' The runes around the glade pulsed with energy, and the fireflies' light intensified, growing brighter and stronger with every second.

Tharion's roar filled the air, his dark magic lashing out in desperation. "No! I will not be defeated!"

Cassian focused on the crystal, his connection to the fireflies solidifying. "This is for Mother. This is for the balance."

The crystal pulsed, and the fireflies' full power was unleashed.

Chapter 18: The Shadow of Fear

The world around them seemed to collapse into darkness as Tharion's full power was unleashed. The sky above the Heart of the Glade twisted and roiled, black clouds swirling in a nightmarish spiral, as if the heavens themselves had turned against them. The fireflies' light flickered wildly, their protective glow faltering as the ancient sorcerer's shadow stretched across the land like a living, breathing entity.

Cassian's heart raced in his chest, the crystal in his hand trembling as the energy around them became suffocating. The air was thick with the smell of burning ash, and the ground beneath their feet cracked and splintered as if the earth itself was breaking apart. The trees surrounding the glade twisted unnaturally, their branches reaching toward the sky like skeletal fingers grasping for salvation that would never come.

Tharion's voice echoed through the air, cold and malicious, sending chills down Cassian's spine. "You are too late," he sneered, his words dripping with venom. "You cannot escape the darkness that awaits you."

Lyra's music faltered for a moment, her breath catching in her throat as she struggled to keep the fireflies' light steady. Her flute shook in her hands, and her normally calm and graceful presence was shaken by the sheer weight of Tharion's power pressing down on them. "It's... too strong," she whispered, her voice barely audible. "I can feel him... pulling me under..."

Cassian turned to his sister, fear gripping his chest as he saw the panic in her eyes. "Lyra! Focus! Do not let him in!" he shouted, though his own voice trembled with the same fear gnawing at his mind. He could feel it too—Tharion's influence creeping into his thoughts, filling his head with whispers, promises of power, and the overwhelming urge to give in.

Orion stood at the front, his blade raised, but even he was starting to falter. His strikes against Tharion's dark energy were becoming slower, weaker, as if something unseen was draining the very life from him. Shadows seemed to cling to his form, swirling around him like a suffocating fog. His breath came in ragged gasps, and he swayed, fighting to stay upright. "Cassian... I... I cannot..." he muttered, his voice barely above a whisper.

The fireflies around them flickered erratically, their light dimming as Tharion's darkness pressed in from all sides. Cassian could feel the ground shift beneath him, cracking and heaving as the sorcerer's magic twisted reality itself. The trees groaned as their branches bent and snapped, their once vibrant leaves curling and blackening as if consumed by an unseen flame.

And then, from the shadows, Cassian saw something that made his blood run cold.

Out of the corner of his eye, dark figures began to emerge—twisted, contorted shapes, barely human. Their faces were pale, hollow-eyed, and stretched into grotesque expressions of terror, their mouths gaping open in silent screams. They moved toward the siblings with jerky, unnatural motions, their arms outstretched as if to drag them into the abyss.

Cassian's breath hitched in his throat as the figures drew closer, their faces becoming more defined, more familiar. "No... it can't be..." His voice was barely a whisper as he recognized them. They were the faces of those who had once been lost to Tharion's darkness—souls trapped in eternal torment, their features twisted into nightmarish mockeries of who they once were.

And there, among them, were the faces of his parents.

"Mother... Father..." Cassian's legs felt like lead, his heart pounding in his chest as he stumbled backward, the sight of his parents' hollowed faces searing into his mind. They reached out toward him, their once loving eyes now filled with a void of nothingness, as if their very souls had been consumed. "This isn't real... it can't be real..."

Tharion's laughter echoed through the glade, deep and cruel. "Oh, but it is, child. They are with me now—forever bound to the darkness. And soon, you will join them."

Cassian felt his knees buckle as the weight of those words crashed over him. His vision blurred as tears stung his eyes, his chest tightening as the horror of it all threatened to consume him. He had fought so hard, they all had, but what if it had all been for nothing? What if this was how it ended—lost in the same darkness that had claimed his parents?

Lyra's scream cut through the haze, sharp and filled with terror. Cassian turned just in time to see her collapse to her knees, her flute falling from her hands as her body trembled uncontrollably. Shadows swirled around her, twisting, and writhing as if they were alive, pulling her down into the earth. Her eyes were wide with fear, her voice hoarse as she cried out for help. "I cannot... I cannot get out..."

Orion's strength faltered as he too was pulled down by the dark tendrils. The shadows wrapped around him, binding him in place, draining his strength with each passing second. His face was pale, and his eyes were wide with disbelief. "It's over," he muttered, his voice weak. "We've already lost..."

Cassian's heart hammered in his chest as he looked at his siblings, seeing the fear in their eyes, the darkness closing in on them. His breath came in shallow, panicked gasps, and the whispers in his mind grew louder, more insistent. Give in, Cassian. You cannot win. Join them. Join the darkness.

But then, from somewhere deep within, a voice—his mother's voice—cut through the noise. You are stronger than this, Cassian. Remember who you are. Remember what you fight for.

The fireflies around him flickered weakly, but they were still there. He could still feel their presence, their magic, their light. And that light, no matter how dim, was enough to push back the darkness.

With a deep breath, Cassian stood up, his legs trembling but holding. He gripped the crystal tightly, feeling its warmth pulse faintly in his hand. "I won't let you win," he said, his voice barely more than a whisper, but growing stronger with each word. "We won't let you win."

He turned to Lyra and Orion, his voice breaking through the suffocating fog of fear that surrounded them. "We are still here! We are still fighting!"

Lyra looked up at him, her eyes wide with fear but flickering with a glimmer of hope. Orion gritted his teeth, forcing himself to stand, though the shadows still clung to him. "We fight together," he growled through clenched teeth.

Cassian raised the crystal, and with it, the fireflies' light flared—weak, but enough. Enough to push back the shadows, enough to give them a chance. "Eldrin, now!" he shouted, his voice echoing through the glade.

Eldrin's light blazed brighter than before, and the fireflies surged forward, their collective glow cutting through the dark tendrils that surrounded them. The twisted, nightmarish figures began to waver, their forms dissolving into smoke as the fireflies' magic pierced the darkness.

Tharion roared in fury, his form twisting and writhing as the fireflies' light pushed against him. "This isn't over!" he bellowed, his voice shaking the very earth beneath them. "You cannot stop me!"

But Cassian stood tall now, his fear replaced by a growing determination. "We can. And we will."

With a final surge of power, the fireflies' light exploded outward, flooding the glade with brilliant, blinding radiance. The shadows recoiled, the dark tendrils snapping and dissolving under the force of the light. Tharion's form wavered, his once-imposing figure now nothing more than a fading shadow.

The nightmare was ending.

Chapter 19: Into the Abyss

The moment the light exploded from the crystal, the world went quiet—unnervingly quiet. The fireflies' radiance had pushed back Tharion's shadow, but the oppressive darkness that lingered in the air seemed thicker, as if reality itself was beginning to fracture under the weight of his magic.

Cassian stumbled forward, his heart pounding in his ears. Every breath wanted to drag air through thick fog, each step heavier than the last. The ground beneath him felt unstable, as if it might give way at any moment, plunging him into the depths below. He could not shake the feeling that they were being watched—stalked by something just out of sight.

"Is it over?" Lyra's voice trembled, her hands clutching her flute like a lifeline. She looked pale, her usually bright eyes now clouded with uncertainty. The fireflies hovered around her, but even their glow seemed faint, barely illuminating the space around them.

"No." Orion's voice was low, grim. His sword was drawn, his knuckles white from the force of his grip. "He is still here. I can feel him. Watching. Waiting."

Cassian swallowed hard, his gaze sweeping the glade. The once-sacred space now looked twisted—warped by Tharion's magic. The trees, once ancient and wise, now loomed like skeletal figures, their branches curling inward, clawing at the sky. Shadows stretched unnaturally, moving even when there was no light to cast them.

A soft, wet sound echoed from the trees, like something dragging itself through the underbrush. Cassian's breath hitched. "What was that?" he whispered, his voice barely audible.

Lyra stepped closer to Cassian, her eyes wide with fear. "I don't know, but it's coming closer."

Orion took a step forward, his sword raised. "Stay close. Whatever it is, we will face it together."

Suddenly, from the darkness between the trees, a figure appeared shambling, twisted, its body bent at unnatural angles. Its skin was pale, glistening like wet stone, and its eyes... its eyes were hollow, gaping pits of nothingness. As it moved, its limbs jerked and twisted, as though it had forgotten how to walk.

Cassian's heart leapt into his throat. "What is that?" he gasped, backing away, his hand instinctively clutching the crystal.

The figure staggered toward them, dragging something behind it—something wet and heavy. Its head jerked to the side, and Cassian saw its mouth... stitched shut, with thick, black thread binding its lips together. It let out a soft, muffled moan, the sound of despair and agony.

Lyra whimpered, her voice barely a whisper. "We have to get out of here."

But the creature was not alone. From the shadows, more figures began to emerge, each more grotesque than the last—some with their faces distorted, their features melted like wax, others with limbs that seemed too long, too thin, like insects crawling toward them on brittle legs. Their skin was mottled with patches of decay, and their eyes—those empty, hollow eyes—were fixed on the siblings.

Orion raised his sword, his jaw clenched. "Stay behind me," he growled, though even he looked shaken by the sight of them. "We need to find a way out."

Cassian's mind raced. *This is not real. This cannot be real.* But no matter how hard he tried to convince himself, the smell of rot, the sound of their dragging limbs—it was all too real.

Tharion's voice slithered through the air, smooth and venomous. "Do you see, children? Do you see what awaits you in the dark? This is the fate of those who thought they could stand against me. Now it is yours."

Cassian's grip tightened on the crystal, his heart pounding in his chest. "We won't end up like them," he shouted, though his voice wavered with fear. "We'll stop you."

Tharion's laugh echoed through the glade, cold and hollow. "Stop me? You cannot even save yourselves."

The figures moved faster now, their twisted forms jerking and twitching as they closed in on the siblings. Their moans grew louder, the sound of their dragging limbs now a chorus of terror. They reached out, long, bony fingers curling as if to grasp at the siblings, to pull them into the abyss.

Orion swung his sword, but even as the blade struck the first creature, it dissolved into a thick, black mist—only to reappear moments later, its body reforming, more twisted and grotesque than before.

"They can't be killed," Lyra cried, her voice filled with panic. "What are they?"

Cassian's pulse raced as he looked down at the crystal in his hand, its light flickering weakly. "The fireflies... they're trying to help, but it's not enough." He turned to his siblings, desperation in his eyes. "We need more light. It is the only thing that can hold them back."

Lyra nodded, her hands shaking as she raised her flute to her lips. Her melody was weak at first, trembling, but as she played, the fireflies around them began to glow brighter, their light pushing back the shadows—if only for a moment.

But the creatures were relentless. They clawed at the light, their bodies twisting and contorting in unnatural ways, as though the very darkness was feeding off their fear.

Cassian's mind spun, his thoughts clouded by the oppressive weight of the darkness. "We have to reach the Heart of the Glade. It is the only way."

Orion grunted as he slashed through another creature, its form dissolving into mist before reforming again. "Then we move. Now."

Together, the siblings sprinted toward the center of the glade, the creatures lunging at them from all sides. Cassian's heart raced as the crystal pulsed weakly in his hand, its light flickering with each step. The fireflies followed, but even their once-brilliant light seemed to struggle against the overwhelming tide of darkness.

As they neared the Heart of the Glade, the ground beneath them began to crack and shift, deep fissures opening in the earth. Cassian stumbled, nearly falling as the ground gave way beneath him. He caught himself just in time, but when he looked up, he saw It—waiting for them.

Tharion.

His form was more monstrous than before, a towering figure of shadow and flame. His eyes burned with malice, and his body seemed to pulse with dark energy, tendrils of black smoke swirling around him like a storm.

"Welcome," Tharion hissed, his voice a venomous whisper. "To your end."

Cassian's heart pounded in his chest as he stared up at the sorcerer, his mind racing with fear and desperation. They were out of time. The darkness was closing in, and Tharion stood between them and their only chance at survival.

But something stirred within Cassian—a spark of defiance. He raised the crystal high, its light flickering one last time. "We're not finished yet."

Tharion's laugh was low, filled with cruel amusement. "Oh, but you are."

The ground beneath them trembled as the last battle began.

Chapter 20: Beneath the Darkened Sky

The sky above the Heart of the Glade had turned into a swirling mass of black clouds, heavy with the weight of impending doom. The air was thick with the scent of ash and decay, as if the very earth were dying beneath their feet. The fireflies hovered close to the siblings, their light flickering with desperation, struggling to pierce the oppressive darkness that surrounded them.

Cassian gripped the crystal tightly in his hand, its weak glow the only thing keeping the encroaching shadows at bay. His heart raced, his pulse pounding in his ears. Tharion stood before them, a towering figure cloaked in shadow, his eyes glowing with a malevolent light that seemed to devour everything around him.

Orion stepped forward, his sword gleaming with what little light remained. His jaw was clenched, his muscles tense as he prepared for the inevitable clash. "This is it," he muttered, his voice low. "This is where we make our stand."

Lyra's hand trembled as she raised her flute to her lips, her eyes fixed on Tharion. "We can't let him take the fireflies' magic," she whispered, her voice quivering with fear. "If he succeeds... everything will be lost."

Tharion's laugh echoed through the glade, deep and mocking, sending chills down Cassian's spine. "Lost?" the sorcerer hissed, his voice filled with cruel amusement. "You think there is anything left to save? This world is already mine."

With a sudden, violent movement, Tharion raised his hand, and the earth beneath the siblings' feet began to quake. Dark tendrils of energy erupted from the ground, twisting, and writhing like serpents, slithering toward them with deadly intent.

"Move!" Orion shouted, leaping out of the way as one of the tendrils snapped toward him, narrowly missing his legs.

Cassian stumbled backward, barely avoiding the tendrils as they lashed out at him, their touch leaving scorched marks on the ground. He could feel the heat emanating from them, the dark energy radiating with a malice that made his skin crawl.

Lyra played a sharp, high-pitched note on her flute, and the fireflies surged toward the tendrils, their light pushing them back—but only for a moment. The darkness seemed to swallow the fireflies' glow, absorbing their light, and growing stronger with each passing second.

Cassian's breath came in ragged gasps as he struggled to keep the crystal steady. "We need more light," he gasped, his voice shaking with fear. "We can't hold him off like this."

Orion gritted his teeth as he swung his sword at one of the tendrils, cutting through it, but it only reformed moments later, thicker, and more menacing. "Then what do we do?" he growled, frustration seeping into his voice. "We're running out of time!"

Tharion's voice slithered through the air like a chilly wind. "You cannot escape the inevitable. Your resistance is nothing more than a fleeting distraction."

Cassian's mind raced as he tried to think of a plan, something—anything—that could turn the tide of the battle. But the darkness was too strong, too overwhelming. Every strike they made seemed to be absorbed, every step they took felt heavier than the last.

The fireflies circled them, their light flickering weakly, and Cassian could feel their fear. He could sense their desperation, their fight to keep the darkness at bay, but they were losing.

Suddenly, a piercing shriek cut through the air—a sound so sharp and unnatural that it made Cassian's blood run cold. He turned just in time to see something rising from the shadows—a figure, tall and thin, its body twisted and contorted like it had been broken and reassembled wrong. Its eyes were hollow, its mouth stretched wide in a silent scream.

"By the light..." Orion whispered, his voice filled with horror.

The creature moved with jerky, unnatural motions, its limbs snapping and twisting as it stumbled toward them. Dark, dripping ooze trailed behind it, staining the ground with each step. More figures emerged from the shadows, each one more grotesque than the last—some crawling on all fours like animals, others dragging themselves along the ground as if their bodies were too broken to stand.

Cassian felt his stomach churn with disgust and fear. The creatures moved with purpose, their empty eyes fixed on the siblings, their movements growing faster and more frenzied with each passing second.

"We have to go," Lyra gasped, her voice trembling as she played another note on her flute, trying to keep the fireflies' light strong.

Orion's sword gleamed as he slashed at the nearest creature, but like the tendrils, it dissolved into mist before reforming moments later. "They keep coming," he growled. "There's no end to them!"

Cassian's mind spun, his heart racing as he looked at the twisted figures closing in on them. The crystal in his hand flickered weakly, and he could feel the fireflies' light fading. "We need to get to the heart of the glade," he said, his voice filled with urgency. "It's our only chance."

Lyra nodded, her breath coming in quick, panicked bursts. "But how? They are everywhere!"

Cassian clenched his teeth, his eyes narrowing as he focused on the crystal. "We have to make a run for it. If we do not..."

He did not finish the sentence. He did not have to.

With a deep breath, Cassian tightened his grip on the crystal and took off toward the center of the glade, his heart pounding in his chest. The ground shook beneath his feet, and the shadows seemed to close in around him, but he did not stop. He could not.

Behind him, he could hear Orion shouting, the sound of his sword cutting through the air, and Lyra's frantic flute notes, but the creatures kept coming, relentless, unstoppable. The shadows twisted and writhed, trying to drag them down, to pull them into the darkness.

Cassian reached the heart of the glade, the stone altar standing at its center, covered in ancient runes that pulsed faintly with what little magic remained. His breath hitched as he saw the darkness creeping up the sides of the altar, trying to consume it, trying to snuff out the last remnants of light.

"Cassian!" Lyra's voice was filled with panic, and he turned just in time to see one of the creatures lunging at her, its long, thin arms reaching out with unnatural speed.

"Get down!" Orion roared, slashing at the creature, but his sword passed through it as though it were made of smoke.

Cassian's pulse quickened as he pressed the crystal to the altar, its light flaring weakly. "Come on," he whispered, his voice shaking. "Come on!"

But nothing happened.

Tharion's voice echoed through the glade, deep and mocking. "It is too late, boy. The fireflies' magic is fading, and soon it will be gone—forever."

Cassian's heart pounded in his chest, his breath coming in ragged gasps. He looked down at the crystal, its light flickering, barely a spark of what it once was.

No. It cannot end like this.

But the shadows were closing in, the creatures drawing nearer, their hollow eyes filled with hunger, their movements growing more erratic, more frenzied.

And then, in that moment of darkness, Cassian felt something—a warmth, faint but real, pulsing from the crystal in his hand.

He looked up, his eyes widening as the runes on the altar began to glow, faint at first, but growing brighter with each passing second.

"Cassian!" Lyra's voice was filled with hope, and he turned to see the fireflies gathering around the altar, their light flaring brightly, pushing back the shadows, the creatures dissolving into mist.

The darkness recoiled, and Tharion let out a furious roar, his form twisting and writhing as the fireflies' magic surged through the glade.

Cassian's grip tightened on the crystal as the light flared, brighter and brighter, until it was blinding.

And then, with a deafening roar, the darkness shattered.

Chapter 21: Cracks in the Light

The world was silent in the wake of the explosion of light. For a moment, all was still. The shadows that had surrounded the siblings were gone, their twisted forms dissolved into nothing. The creatures that had clawed at them had vanished, leaving only the faint scent of decay in the air. The oppressive darkness that had weighed on their souls lifted, replaced by a fragile, trembling peace.

Cassian stumbled forward, his vision blurred by the blinding light that had erupted from the crystal. His chest heaved as he struggled to catch his breath, his heart pounding in his ears. The fireflies still hovered around him, their glow bright and steady, but something felt wrong—like the calm before a storm.

"Is it over?" Lyra's voice was a trembling whisper as she stepped closer to him, her flute hanging limply at her side. Her eyes were wide, her face pale with exhaustion and fear. "Did we stop him?"

Orion stood a few steps ahead, his sword still drawn, though his grip had loosened. He scanned the clearing, his gaze sharp and wary. "I don't know," he muttered, his voice low. "I don't think this is over."

Cassian could feel it too—the sense that something was still lurking, waiting in the shadows just beyond their reach. His hand tightened around the crystal, but its glow had faded again, now no more than a faint flicker of light. The fireflies around him buzzed softly, their energy diminished but not extinguished.

Suddenly, the ground beneath their feet trembled—a soft, ominous rumble that sent a chill down Cassian's spine. He looked around, his heart sinking as he saw cracks begin to form in the earth, spreading out from the altar at the heart of the glade like the web of a spider. The runes that had glowed so brightly moments before now flickered, as if the magic were struggling to hold on.

Lyra took a step back, her eyes darting to the cracks in the ground. "What's happening?" she asked, her voice shaking. "Why is it... why does it feel like it's falling apart?"

Orion moved closer to the altar, his face grim. "Because it is."

Cassian's breath caught in his throat as the realization hit him. The light from the fireflies had shattered the darkness, but it had not destroyed it. It had only weakened it, driven it back. And now, the darkness was coming for them again, creeping in through the cracks in the earth, waiting for its chance to strike.

A low, rumbling growl echoed through the glade, vibrating in the air around them. It was a sound that Cassian had heard before, in his nightmares—the voice of something ancient, something filled with malice and hunger. He felt the hair on the back of his neck stand on end as a chilly wind swept through the trees, carrying with it the scent of rot and decay.

"We need to move," Orion said, his voice sharp. "Now."

But before they could take a step, the ground beneath them gave way, crumbling into a deep, dark chasm. The world seemed to tilt, and for a heart-stopping moment, Cassian felt weightless, as if he were falling into an endless void.

He hit the ground hard, the impact jarring his bones. Pain shot through his limbs as he scrambled to his feet, his heart racing. The glade was gone, swallowed by the darkness below. The sky above was nothing more than a swirling mass of black clouds, and the air was thick with the stench of death.

"Cassian!" Lyra's voice rang out, frantic and high-pitched. She was nearby, struggling to get up from where she had fallen. Her flute had rolled away, and her hands shook as she tried to reach for it.

"I'm here!" Cassian called out, his voice tight with fear. He staggered toward her, his legs feeling like lead as he moved through the thick, cloying air.

Orion was on his feet, his sword drawn once more. His face was pale, but his eyes were sharp with determination. "Stay close," he ordered, his voice low but firm. "We don't know what's down here."

Cassian glanced around, his heart pounding in his chest. The darkness felt alive, pressing in from all sides, suffocating them. Shadows moved in the distance, twisting, and shifting like living creatures, watching them with eyes that glowed faintly in the dark.

"This... this is wrong," Lyra whispered, her voice barely audible. "This place... it feels like it's alive."

Orion nodded, his gaze fixed on the shadows. "We need to get out of here," he said through gritted teeth. "We cannot fight down here. Not like this."

Cassian's hand tightened around the crystal, but its light had dimmed almost completely. He could feel the fireflies' energy, but it was weak, fading. "The crystal... it's not enough," he muttered, his voice filled with frustration.

A low, deep laugh echoed through the chasm, cold and mocking. Tharion's voice. "You cannot run from the dark, children. It is everywhere. It is within you."

The shadows around them began to move, creeping closer with each passing second. Cassian felt his heart race as he saw shapes forming in the dark—twisted, contorted figures that slithered and crawled, their eyes gleaming with malevolence.

"Cassian!" Lyra's voice was sharp with panic as one of the figures lunged toward her, its long, thin fingers reaching out with impossible speed.

Before Cassian could react, Orion stepped forward, his sword flashing as he slashed at the creature. The blade passed through it, but the figure reformed almost instantly, its body twisting and writhing like smoke.

"They can't be killed," Orion growled, his eyes narrowing. "We need to get out of here—now."

Cassian's pulse raced as he looked around for an escape, but the chasm seemed endless, the shadows closing in from all sides. The fireflies buzzed weakly around him, their light flickering as if they were barely holding on.

A voice echoed in his mind, faint but clear—his mother's voice. Cassian... trust the light.

His heart pounded in his chest as he closed his eyes, focusing on the crystal in his hand. The fireflies' energy was faint, but it was still there, still fighting. He could feel their fear, their desperation, but also their hope—their belief in the light.

"We can't run," he said, his voice steady despite the fear clawing at his mind. "We have to stand and fight."

Orion's eyes flickered with uncertainty. "Fight what? These shadows... they are endless."

Cassian looked at the crystal, his mind racing. "Not the shadows. Tharion. We have to face him."

Lyra's eyes widened, her face pale. "Are you mad? We cannot—"

But before she could finish, the ground beneath them shifted again, and the darkness surged forward, wrapping around them like a living thing. Cassian felt the air leave his lungs as the shadows closed in, suffocating him, pulling him deeper into the abyss.

And then, all at once, the fireflies' light flared.

It was not bright—not like before—but it was enough. The shadows recoiled, hissing as they shrank away from the light, their forms dissolving into the air.

Cassian gasped for breath, his heart pounding in his chest. The light flickered again, weak but steady, and the shadows retreated, leaving them standing alone in the darkness.

"We have to find him," Cassian whispered, his voice barely audible. "It's the only way."

Orion nodded, his jaw clenched. "Then we do it together."

The fireflies hovered around them, their light dim but persistent, guiding them forward. The darkness loomed all around, but they moved together, stepping into the heart of the abyss.

Chapter 22: The Siege Begins

The journey back to the Citadel was quiet, but the air was thick with tension. Cassian, Lyra, and Orion moved quickly through the forest, their hearts racing with the knowledge that something was terribly wrong. They could feel it—an unease, a dark presence pressing in on them as they neared their home. The fireflies hovered close, their light flickering anxiously as if sensing the same threat.

The Citadel, once a place of safety and protection, loomed ahead of them, its towering stone walls dark against the twilight sky. But something was off. The usual glow of the Citadel's magical wards, the gentle hum of its protective spells, was dimmed. Cassian felt a knot of fear tighten in his chest.

"We need to hurry," he muttered, quickening his pace. "Something's wrong."

Orion glanced at him, his brow furrowed. "I feel it too. The Citadel's defenses... they are weakening."

Lyra's face was pale, her eyes wide with worry. "Do you think Tharion...?"

Before she could finish her sentence, a deafening crack split the air, followed by a rumble that shook the ground beneath their feet. Cassian's heart leapt into his throat as he looked up, his eyes widening in horror.

Above the Citadel, dark clouds swirled ominously, lightning crackling through the sky. Shadows stretched across the stone walls, twisting, and writhing like living things. From the heart of the Citadel, a dark, pulsing energy radiated outward, corrupting the magical wards that had once protected it.

"He's here," Cassian whispered, his voice filled with dread. "Tharion is attacking the Citadel."

Without another word, the siblings sprinted toward the gates, their hearts pounding in their chests. As they drew closer, they could see the chaos unfolding within the Citadel's walls. Luminaires were running in every direction, their faces filled with panic as dark figures emerged from the shadows, creatures of nightmare and malice that clawed and tore at anything in their path.

The Citadel, once a place of order and sanctuary, had become a battleground.

"We have to get inside!" Orion shouted, his sword already drawn as he slashed at one of the dark creatures that lunged toward them from the shadows. The creature hissed, its body dissolving into smoke, only to reform moments later.

Cassian's mind raced as he dodged another attack, his grip tightening around the crystal in his hand. The fireflies buzzed around him, their light flickering as they tried to hold back the darkness. "We need to find the council," he said, his voice tight with urgency. "We need to know how to stop this."

Lyra nodded, her flute in hand as she played a sharp, frantic melody, the fireflies responding to her call. Their light flared, pushing back the shadows for a brief moment, but Cassian could see that it would not hold for long.

The siblings fought their way through the chaos, moving deeper into the Citadel as dark tendrils of Tharion's magic clawed at the walls. The air was thick with the scent of burning magic, and the once-familiar halls now felt foreign, twisted by the corrupting energy that had seeped into the very stone.

As they reached the central chamber where the council usually met, Cassian's heart sank. The doors had been blown off their hinges, and inside, the chamber was filled with dark smoke. The bodies of fallen Luminaires littered the floor, their faces twisted in terror.

"No..." Lyra whispered, her voice breaking. She stumbled forward, her hands shaking as she knelt beside one of the fallen. "They're... gone."

Orion clenched his fists, his jaw tight with rage. "Tharion is destroying everything," he growled. "We have to stop him before there's nothing left."

Cassian's mind raced as he looked around the chamber, his eyes landing on the central dais where the council had once stood. The air around the dais was thick with dark magic, and at its center, a swirling vortex of shadow pulsed, filling the room with a deep, malevolent hum.

"That's it," he muttered, his heart pounding. "That's the source of the corruption."

Orion's gaze hardened as he stepped forward, his sword at the ready. "We destroy it."

But before they could move, a figure emerged from the shadows at the far end of the chamber. Tall and cloaked in darkness, the figure's eyes glowed with a malevolent light. It was Tharion.

"You think you can stop me, children of Evelyn?" Tharion's voice was low, filled with cruel amusement. "The Citadel is mine now. Its magic is mine. And soon, the fireflies' power will be mine as well."

Cassian's heart raced as he stood frozen in place, the weight of Tharion's presence pressing down on him like a suffocating blanket. His breath came in shallow gasps as he struggled to focus, the fireflies around him flickering weakly as if they, too, were being overwhelmed by the sorcerer's dark magic.

"We won't let you destroy everything," Orion snarled, stepping forward, his sword gleaming in the dim light. "We'll stop you."

Tharion laughed, the sound echoing through the chamber like the toll of a death knell. "Stop me? You are too late. The Citadel has fallen. And soon, you will fall with it."

The shadows around Tharion twisted and writhed, forming into monstrous shapes that slithered toward the siblings, their mouths open in silent screams. Cassian felt a wave of terror wash over him as the creatures closed in, their twisted forms barely visible in the dark.

"We have to do something," Lyra cried, her voice filled with desperation. "We can't let him take the Citadel!"

Cassian gritted his teeth, his mind racing as he looked at the crystal in his hand. The fireflies' light was fading, but it was not gone—not yet. He could still feel their magic, still feel their hope.

"We have to destroy the vortex," he said, his voice steady despite the fear clawing at his mind. "It's the only way to stop the corruption."

Orion nodded, his gaze fixed on the swirling mass of shadow at the center of the room. "Then we fight."

With a surge of determination, the siblings charged toward the vortex, their weapons raised, their hearts filled with the fireflies' fading light. The shadows lunged at them, their twisted forms blocking their path, but they pressed on, their resolve unshakable.

Cassian could feel the darkness closing in around them, the weight of Tharion's magic pressing down on him like a physical force. But he would not give up. Not now.

As they neared the vortex, the fireflies around them flared, their light pushing back the darkness for a brief, fleeting moment. Cassian raised the crystal high, the fireflies' magic surging through him as he prepared to strike.

"This is for the Citadel," he whispered, his voice filled with determination. "And for everyone, we've lost."

With a final, desperate push, he thrust the crystal into the heart of the vortex.

The room exploded with light.

Chapter 23: The Fall of Light

The moment Cassian drove the crystal into the vortex, the light burst forth in a violent, blinding flash. For a split second, the shadows that had smothered the Citadel peeled back, like night retreating from dawn. But as quickly as the light came, it flickered—then died, leaving the chamber swallowed by a thick, choking darkness.

Cassian gasped, his heart hammering in his chest. The crystal, once a beacon of hope, now felt cold and lifeless in his hand. The swirling mass of shadows at the heart of the Citadel had not faded. If anything, the vortex had grown darker, its edges rippling as though it had been feeding off their attack.

The dark figures that encircled them lurched closer, their forms barely human, their twisted limbs jerking and twitching with unnatural hunger. Their mouths hung open in silent screams, and their hollow eyes glowed faintly in the darkness, fixed on the siblings like predators to prey.

"No," Lyra's voice broke, trembling as she stared at the creatures closing in. "It did not work... It did not stop him..."

Orion stood in front of her, sword raised, his knuckles white with tension. His eyes darted between the creatures and Tharion, whose figure loomed larger and more malevolent with every passing second. "We are running out of time. If we do not stop this, the Citadel is going to collapse."

But even his voice wavered with doubt. The air had become thick and oppressive, every breath tasting like ash and decay. The ground beneath their feet trembled as cracks spider-webbed across the stone, leaking tendrils of black smoke.

Tharion's laugh was deep, resonating through the chamber like a death knell. His eyes gleamed with malevolent joy, and as he stepped forward, the very air seemed to warp around him, distorting reality. "Did you really think you could challenge me with the magic of these insects?" His voice dripped with cruelty, his form shifting like a shadow made of nightmares. "You've only delayed the inevitable."

Cassian felt his breath catch in his throat. The fireflies—once their only hope—flickered weakly around him. He could feel their energy fading, as if they were being slowly drained by the dark magic that permeated every corner of the Citadel. His pulse quickened as dread washed over him. We are losing...

The shadows crawled closer, their twisted, grotesque forms becoming more defined in the dim light. Limbs too long and misshapen to be human, faces that looked like they had been melted and reformed wrong. Their mouths hung open in grotesque silence, yet Cassian could feel their screams, echoing in his mind. They dragged themselves toward the siblings with jerky, unnatural movements, fingers clawing at the stone floor, leaving deep, black marks behind.

One of the creatures lurched toward Lyra, its elongated fingers wrapping around her wrist like ice-cold steel. Her scream pierced the suffocating air as she tried to pull free, but the creature's grip tightened, dragging her down, its hollow eyes fixed on her, filled with an endless, ravenous hunger.

"Cassian!" she screamed, terror ripping through her voice. "Help me!"

Cassian moved without thinking, his heart pounding in his ears as he swung the crystal at the creature, but the moment the crystal touched its form, the figure dissolved into thick, black mist—only to reform seconds later, its grip stronger, more determined.

"We can't kill them," Orion growled, slashing at another figure that had appeared from the shadows. His sword cut through the air, but the creature reformed just as quickly, its mouth stretching wide in a soundless laugh. "They are not real. They are... they are nightmares."

Tharion's presence grew heavier, the air itself warping and twisting around him as he moved closer. His voice was cold, devoid of life. "You still do not understand. The Citadel is already mine. You are fighting shadows... echoes of a power you will never comprehend."

Cassian's hands shook as he looked at the crystal, its light now barely a flicker. His mind raced, but no solution came. The fireflies, their once-brilliant glow, were dying. The vortex—its center now a massive, burning eye—stared down at them from the heart of the chamber, a malevolent presence beyond anything Cassian had ever imagined.

A low, guttural growl echoed from the vortex, a sound so deep it seemed to rattle the very bones of the Citadel. Cassian's breath caught in his throat as he saw something stir within the swirling shadows—something enormous, something monstrous. The eye blinked slowly, its gaze fixating on them with a cold, inhuman hunger.

Lyra's breath hitched, her voice barely a whisper. "What... what is that?"

Orion's grip tightened on his sword, but for the first time, his face showed true fear. "It's not just Tharion," he muttered, his voice low and tense. "There is something else in there. Something ancient. Something worse."

Cassian's heart pounded in his chest as the vortex pulsed, dark tendrils of shadow stretching out toward them. Every instinct in his body screamed to run, but there was nowhere to go. The Citadel's walls were collapsing, the ceiling cracking as dark magic seeped into every crevice.

A new wave of dark figures emerged from the shadows, their forms even more grotesque than before. Limbs twisted in impossible ways, faces contorted into expressions of pure torment. Their empty eyes gleamed with a sickening hunger, and they moved faster now, closing in with a speed that made Cassian's blood run cold.

"We need more light," Cassian gasped, his voice shaking as he struggled to hold the crystal steady. "The fireflies... there is more power, I can feel it, but we have to reach it. We have to—"

Tharion's laugh cut through the air like a blade. "You think the fireflies can save you?" His voice was a sneer, filled with disdain. "Their magic is weak, dying. Like you."

Cassian's pulse quickened as his grip tightened on the crystal. The fireflies' energy was faint, but it was still there. He could feel their magic pulsing beneath the surface, weak but not gone. There is still hope. There has to be.

"We can't run," he said, his voice trembling but steady. "We have to face him. We have to close the vortex."

Lyra's hands shook as she raised her flute to her lips, her eyes filled with determination despite the terror in her gaze. "Then let's do it."

As she played, the haunting melody filled the chamber, resonating through the stone walls like a ghostly echo. The fireflies responded, their light flaring weakly as they gathered around the siblings, their energy surging toward the crystal.

Cassian closed his eyes, focusing on the fireflies' magic. He could feel their power, buried deep, like a spark struggling to ignite. We can do this. We have to.

The crystal in his hand began to glow, its light growing brighter with each passing second. The fireflies' magic surged, pushing back the shadows, their light flaring as they fought against Tharion's overwhelming darkness.

For a moment, hope surged in Cassian's chest. The fireflies' light was pushing back the creatures, forcing them to retreat, their twisted forms dissolving into mist.

But then, from deep within the vortex, the massive eye blinked again—and the ground shook violently. A wave of dark energy exploded from the center of the vortex, slamming into them with a force that sent Cassian flying backward. His body hit the stone wall with a sickening crack, the air knocked from his lungs as pain shot through him.

The crystal slipped from his grasp, skittering across the floor as the fireflies' light flickered—then went dark.

Cassian's vision blurred as he struggled to stay conscious, his body screaming in pain. Lyra's scream pierced the darkness, filled with terror as the shadows closed in around them.

And then, the light was gone.

The chamber was swallowed by darkness, and the last sound Cassian heard was Tharion's cold, triumphant laugh echoing in the void.

Chapter 24: Beneath the Shadows

Cassian woke to an unbearable silence, a silence so heavy it felt as though the world itself had ceased to exist. His body ached, pain radiating from every joint, but it was the crushing weight on his chest that stole his breath. The darkness was so thick, so all-encompassing, it felt like it was pressing into his skin, sinking into his bones.

The fireflies' light was gone.

He reached out blindly, his fingers brushing against cold stone, slick with something wet—something that made his stomach turn. His heart raced as panic clawed at his throat. Where is the crystal? Where's Lyra? Orion?

The last thing he remembered was the explosion of dark energy, the searing pain of being thrown against the wall, and the sound of Lyra's scream before everything went black.

He forced himself to sit up, wincing as his ribs protested with sharp, stabbing pain. His vision was nothing but an endless, suffocating void. There was no light, no sound—only the oppressive feeling of being trapped in something far beyond his understanding.

"Lyra?" His voice came out like a croak, barely louder than a whisper. He tried again, louder this time. "Orion?"

No response. Just the dark, unyielding silence.

Cassian's heart pounded in his chest as he fumbled blindly, his hands shaking. The crystal—he needed the crystal. It had to be somewhere. If he could just find it, maybe he could bring back the light. Maybe the fireflies were not completely gone.

His fingers scraped across the rough stone floor, searching desperately. His breath came in shallow, panicked bursts. Do not give up. Do not let the darkness win.

Then, his hand brushed against something cold, smooth—the crystal.

Cassian's breath hitched as he gripped it tightly, hope sparking in his chest. But as he held it, he realized the crystal was no longer glowing. Its surface, once warm and pulsing with energy, was now cold, lifeless. A hollow weight settled in his stomach.

The fireflies' magic was gone.

"No," he whispered, his voice trembling. "No, no, no..."

A sudden sound broke the silence—a soft, wet dragging noise that sent a chill racing down his spine. It was faint, barely audible, but it was there. Something was moving in the dark. Something was coming.

Cassian froze, his pulse hammering in his ears. The noise grew louder, closer. It sounded like something scraping across the stone floor, something heavy, slow... deliberate.

His breath caught in his throat as the sound stopped, just inches away from him.

And then he heard it—a soft, ragged breath, too close, far too close. He could feel its presence, the cold, unnatural energy radiating from whatever was lurking just beyond the reach of his senses.

It is here.

Cassian's hand tightened around the crystal, his body trembling with fear. He did not dare move, did not dare breathe. Whatever was in the dark, it was waiting. Watching.

For a long, agonizing moment, there was nothing but silence.

Then, from the darkness, a voice—low, twisted, barely human. "You... cannot escape..."

Cassian's blood turned to ice. The voice was so close, as if the speaker were right next to him, whispering in his ear. He could feel the weight of its words pressing into his skull, filling his mind with dread.

His heart raced as he scrambled backward, his body screaming in protest as he moved. But no matter how far he crawled, the darkness pressed in on him, unrelenting, suffocating.

Suddenly, he felt something cold brush against his ankle—a hand, skeletal and twisted. He kicked out, panic taking over, but the grip tightened, pulling him down.

"No!" Cassian shouted, thrashing wildly. His foot connected with something solid, and the grip loosened, but only for a moment. The hand returned, stronger this time, dragging him deeper into the darkness.

He clawed at the stone floor, his fingers scraping against the rough surface, but it was no use. The darkness was pulling him down, pulling him into the abyss.

And then he heard the voice again, closer now, almost inside his head. "You belong to the shadows..."

The cold touch of the hand was everywhere now, crawling up his legs, his arms, wrapping around his chest like a vice. Cassian gasped for air, his lungs burning as the weight of the darkness pressed in from all sides.

This is how it ends. The thought crept into his mind, unbidden. This is where I die.

But just as the darkness seemed ready to consume him completely, a flicker of light—a single, faint pulse from the crystal in his hand.

Cassian's eyes widened as he stared at the crystal, its glow weak but present. The fireflies' magic was not completely gone.

With a surge of desperation, he clung to that light, focusing all of his energy on it, wishing it to grow stronger. The cold grip around him loosened, and for the first time since waking in the darkness, he felt a sliver of hope.

"No," he whispered through gritted teeth. "I won't let you take me."

The crystal pulsed again, brighter this time, and the darkness recoiled, hissing as it retreated. Cassian pushed himself up, gasping for breath as the weight lifted from his chest.

The light from the crystal was weak, barely enough to see by, but it was enough. Enough to push back the shadows.

"Lyra," he called out again, his voice stronger this time. "Orion! Where are you?"

A groan came from somewhere to his right, faint but unmistakable. "Cassian..." It was Orion's voice, weak but alive.

Cassian scrambled toward the sound, his heart racing as the faint glow from the crystal illuminated the space around him. The chamber was still cloaked in shadow, but the light revealed just enough—Orion, slumped against the wall, his sword lying beside him, and Lyra, curled up nearby, her face pale and streaked with dirt.

"We're not done yet," Cassian muttered, his grip tightening on the crystal. "We're still here."

But even as he said the words, the darkness pressed in again, circling them like a predator stalking its prey.

And somewhere, deep within the shadows, the voice returned, whispering in the darkness. "You cannot escape..."

Chapter 25: Whispers in the Dark

The faint glow from the crystal flickered weakly, casting long, distorted shadows on the cracked stone walls of the chamber. Every pulse of light revealed just how far the Citadel had fallen. Once a place of strength and sanctuary, it was now a hollowed-out shell, consumed by darkness. The stone itself seemed to weep with a black, viscous substance, seeping into the cracks and corners like a disease.

Cassian crouched beside Orion and Lyra, his breath shallow as he fought to stay calm. The darkness was alive, he could feel it—pressing against his skin, curling into his mind, whispering that it was all hopeless. But the crystal's faint light, weak as it was, kept those voices at bay. For now.

"We need to get out of here," Orion muttered, his voice strained as he forced himself to sit up. His eyes were bloodshot, his face pale. "This place... it's feeding on us."

Lyra shivered, her arms wrapped around herself, her flute clutched tightly in her hands. "It is not just the Citadel. It is everywhere." Her voice trembled, and Cassian could see the fear in her eyes, the same fear that gnawed at him. "I can feel it... something watching us, waiting for us to slip."

Cassian nodded, his hand tightening around the crystal. The fireflies' magic was barely holding on, and every flicker of light felt like it could be the last. He glanced around, his gaze darting between the shadows that writhed and twisted at the edges of the light. He knew they were not alone—there was something in the dark with them.

"We have to move," he said, his voice low but steady. "We cannot stay here. The longer we wait, the stronger it gets."

Orion pushed himself to his feet, wincing as he grabbed his sword. "Move where? Everything is gone. The Citadel's defenses are broken, and the fireflies are barely hanging on."

Cassian's mind raced as he looked at the crystal. There was still magic inside, still power, but it was slipping away. If they did not find a way to reignite the fireflies' light soon, they would be swallowed by the darkness.

"There's got to be a way to restore the fireflies," he muttered, more to himself than to anyone else. "Something deeper. Something stronger."

Lyra's eyes flickered with a glimmer of hope, though it was faint. "The Heart of the Citadel... where the fireflies' magic was born. If we can get there, maybe we can find a way to bring them back."

Orion frowned, his expression skeptical. "If Tharion hasn't destroyed it already."

Cassian shook his head. "No. I can feel it. The fireflies' power is still connected to the Heart. If we can reach it, we might have a chance."

A sudden, sharp crack echoed through the chamber, reverberating off the stone walls. The siblings froze, their breath catching in their throats. Cassian felt the hairs on the back of his neck stand on end as the sound grew louder and closer.

Footsteps.

Slow, deliberate, echoing through the darkness.

Lyra's eyes widened, her voice barely a whisper. "Someone's here..."

Orion gripped his sword tightly, stepping in front of his siblings as the footsteps drew nearer. The shadows at the edge of the light seemed to ripple, pulling back as something moved through them.

Cassian's heart raced as he strained to see into the darkness, but the light from the crystal was too weak, too dim. The footsteps were slow, measured, as if whoever—or whatever—was approaching wanted them to hear.

"Show yourself!" Orion barked, his voice harsh in the oppressive silence.

For a moment, there was nothing. The footsteps stopped.

Then, from the darkness, a voice—low, deep, and familiar. "You think you can escape the shadows, but they are already inside you."

Cassian's blood ran cold. Tharion.

The shadows began to stir, moving like liquid around the chamber, slithering along the walls, twisting, and curling toward the light. Cassian's breath came in ragged gasps as the dark energy pulsed around them, seeping into the cracks in the stone, warping the very air.

"You are fighting a war you cannot win," Tharion's voice echoed, seeming to come from everywhere at once. "The Citadel is already mine. Your light... is fading."

Lyra's hands shook as she raised her flute, her eyes filled with desperation. "We have to stop him. We cannot let him take everything."

But before she could play, the shadows surged forward, slamming into them with the force of a tidal wave. The crystal's light sputtered and dimmed as the darkness wrapped around them, thick and suffocating.

Cassian gasped for air as he felt the cold tendrils of shadow coil around his arms, his chest, pulling him down. His vision blurred, his mind fogging as the weight of the darkness pressed into him, whispering in his ear. You are too late. You have already lost.

Orion swung his sword wildly, but the blade passed through the shadows like smoke. His movements grew slower, weaker, as the darkness closed in around him.

Lyra's flute slipped from her hands as she fell to her knees, her breath coming in short, panicked bursts. "It's too strong... we can't..."

"No," Cassian gasped, his grip on the crystal tightening even as the darkness tried to tear it from his hands. "We're not done yet."

But the shadows were relentless, their twisted forms writhing and shifting as they crawled toward the light, suffocating it. The sound of Tharion's laughter echoed through the chamber, cold and mocking.

Cassian's vision blurred as the darkness closed in around him, but just as the last flicker of light began to fade, he felt something stir inside the crystal—a faint pulse of energy, weak but persistent.

The fireflies were still there, still fighting.

With a surge of determination, Cassian focused on that pulse, wishing it to grow stronger. He could feel the fireflies' magic, faint but burning like a spark in the darkness. "We have to reach the Heart," he muttered through gritted teeth. "It's the only way."

Orion, barely able to stand, nodded weakly. "Then let us move. Before the shadows finish us."

Cassian forced himself to his feet, his legs trembling as he fought against the weight of the darkness. The crystal in his hand pulsed faintly, the fireflies' magic barely holding on, but it was enough to push back the shadows—just enough to give them a chance.

"We head for the Heart," Cassian said, his voice filled with grim determination. "And we fight until the very end."

Together, the siblings pushed through the suffocating darkness, the faint light from the crystal guiding them toward what could be their final stand. Every step felt like a battle, every breath a struggle against the overwhelming power of Tharion's magic.

But they moved forward, even as the shadows circled, even as Tharion's voice whispered in their ears, promising them that it was all for nothing.

And as they neared the Heart of the Citadel, they could feel it—the pulse of ancient magic, buried deep beneath the stone. The fireflies' last hope.

But Tharion was waiting.

Chapter 26: The Heart of the Citadel

The stone corridors twisted before them, dark and suffocating, as if the very walls of the Citadel had come alive, groaning, and shifting under the weight of the malevolent force that gripped them. Each step felt heavier than the last, the darkness thickening, pulling at their limbs like a thousand invisible hands dragging them toward oblivion. The only thing keeping them moving was the faint, pulsing light of the crystal in Cassian's hand—a weak spark, barely enough to keep the shadows at bay.

"We're close," Cassian whispered, though the words felt hollow in the oppressive silence. He could feel the fireflies' magic pulsing faintly ahead, a thin thread of hope in the heart of the darkness. "The Heart of the Citadel... it's just ahead."

Orion grunted in response, his face pale and lined with exhaustion. His sword hung limply at his side, the weight of the battle wearing him down. "We do not have much time. The longer we stay here, the stronger he gets."

Lyra's eyes were wide with fear, her hands trembling as she clutched her flute. "He is waiting for us... I can feel him. Tharion... he knows we are coming."

Cassian's heart pounded in his chest, his grip tightening on the crystal. The fireflies' magic was barely holding on, flickering like a dying flame, and with each step they took, the shadows pressed closer, darker, and more twisted than before. It was as though the Citadel itself was being consumed by the darkness, its ancient magic rotting away under Tharion's influence.

The corridor opened into a vast chamber, and Cassian's breath caught in his throat.

The Heart of the Citadel lay before them, a massive, ancient structure carved from the stone itself. Its surface was covered in intricate runes, glowing faintly with the last vestiges of the fireflies' magic. But the heart of the structure—once bright and filled with life—was dark, pulsing with a malevolent energy that made Cassian's skin crawl.

Tendrils of black mist twisted around the Heart, seeping into its cracks and crevices, corrupting the magic that had once flowed freely. The shadows danced and writhed across the floor, moving like liquid, whispering, and hissing as they reached out toward the siblings.

Orion's grip tightened on his sword, his voice grim. "He's already corrupted it."

Cassian swallowed hard, his eyes fixed on the dark tendrils that wound their way through the Heart. "Not completely," he muttered. "The fireflies' magic is still there... we just have to reach it."

But as they stepped closer, the shadows surged forward, their forms shifting and solidifying into grotesque, twisted figures. Their bodies were long and thin, their limbs unnaturally elongated, and their faces were nothing more than hollow pits where eyes should have been. They moved with a jerky, unnatural motion, their heads twitching and turning in sharp, inhuman movements as they advanced.

Lyra gasped, stumbling back as the creatures closed in, their mouths opening in silent screams. "We can't fight them," she whispered, her voice trembling. "They're too strong..."

Cassian's pulse quickened as the creatures moved closer, their hollow eyes fixed on them. "We don't have a choice," he said through gritted teeth. "We have to get to the Heart."

Before they could move, a deep, echoing voice filled the chamber, low and cold. "You are too late."

Cassian's heart sank as Tharion's form materialized from the shadows, his presence suffocating. His body seemed to shift and twist like smoke, his eyes glowing with a dark, unnatural light that made the air around him crackle with energy.

"You think you can save the Citadel?" Tharion's voice was filled with cruel amusement as he stepped toward them, his shadow stretching across the chamber. "The fireflies' magic is broken. Their light is dying."

Orion raised his sword, his jaw clenched. "We're not going to let you destroy everything."

Tharion's laughter echoed through the chamber, cold and mocking. "You cannot stop what has already begun."

Cassian's grip on the crystal tightened as he stepped forward, his heart racing. The fireflies' magic was still there—he could feel it, faint but burning like a small flame in the darkness. They were so close, but Tharion's presence was overwhelming, suffocating.

"We can still stop him," Cassian muttered, though his voice wavered with fear. "We just need to get to the Heart."

But before they could move, Tharion raised his hand, and the shadows surged forward, slamming into them with the force of a storm. Cassian was thrown back, his body crashing into the stone floor, the air knocked from his lungs. The crystal skittered across the floor, its light dimming as the shadows wrapped around it, choking the magic within.

Orion staggered to his feet, slashing at the shadows with his sword, but the creatures reformed as quickly as he struck them down, their twisted forms growing stronger with every second.

Lyra scrambled back, her breath coming in panicked gasps as the shadows closed in around her, their hollow eyes gleaming with hunger. She raised her flute to her lips, playing a frantic melody, but the sound was weak, barely enough to push the darkness back.

"We're losing," she cried, her voice filled with desperation. "We can't hold them off."

Cassian's heart pounded in his chest as he struggled to stand, his body aching from the impact. The fireflies' magic was slipping away, and the shadows were growing stronger, feeding off the darkness that pulsed from Tharion's form.

"We have to get to the Heart," Cassian said through gritted teeth, his voice filled with urgency. "It's the only way."

But as they moved forward, Tharion's laughter filled the chamber, and the shadows surged again, more violent than before. Cassian gasped as the darkness wrapped around his legs, pulling him down, dragging him toward the center of the chamber where the Heart lay, its once-bright magic now corrupted.

"You are mine," Tharion hissed, his voice low and filled with malice. "You belong to the darkness."

Cassian's vision blurred as the shadows tightened their grip, his body growing cold as the weight of the darkness pressed in on him. He could feel the fireflies' magic slipping away, their light fading with each passing second.

"No," he whispered, his voice barely audible. "We're not finished."

With a surge of determination, Cassian focused on the crystal, wishing it to glow brighter, willing the fireflies' magic to return. The crystal flickered weakly, but it was not enough. The darkness was too strong.

Orion swung his sword wildly, trying to cut through the shadows that had wrapped around him, but his movements were sluggish, weakened by the weight of the dark magic. Lyra's flute fell from her hands as she collapsed to the ground, her body trembling as the shadows pulled her closer to the Heart.

"Don't give up," Cassian gasped, his voice filled with desperation. "We're not done yet."

But even as he said the words, the darkness closed in around them, suffocating, relentless. Tharion's presence filled the chamber, his power overwhelming, and Cassian could feel the light slipping away.

The fireflies' magic was dying.

And for the first time, Cassian felt the cold grip of defeat.

Chapter 27: Whispers of Betrayal

The shadows seemed to grow thicker with each passing second, clinging to the walls of the chamber like a living, breathing entity. Cassian's body ached from the weight of the darkness pressing down on him, but he forced himself to stand, his hand gripping the crystal tightly. The fireflies' magic flickered weakly, barely holding back the overwhelming tide of Tharion's influence.

Lyra and Orion staggered to their feet beside him, both breathing heavily, their faces pale with exhaustion. The battle had taken its toll, and the dark tendrils that wrapped around the Heart of the Citadel seemed to pulse with life, growing stronger by the minute.

"We're running out of time," Orion muttered, his voice hoarse. "If we don't stop him soon, the fireflies' magic will be gone."

Cassian nodded, his mind racing as he searched for a solution. But something felt wrong—deeply wrong. The shadows were closing in too fast, the Citadel's defenses falling apart too easily. It was almost as if Tharion had known every step they would take.

Suddenly, the sound of footsteps echoed through the chamber, and the siblings turned, their hearts pounding.

From the shadows at the far end of the room, a figure emerged—tall, cloaked, and familiar.

"Master Eryndor?" Cassian's voice wavered as the Luminaire elder stepped into the weak light of the crystal. The sight of him should have brought relief, but instead, it filled Cassian with a cold sense of dread. Eryndor's face was gaunt, his eyes hollow, and there was something about his presence that felt... off.

Orion's hand tightened around his sword, his eyes narrowing. "What are you doing here?"

Eryndor's voice was calm, almost too calm. "I have come to help, of course. The fireflies' magic is fading... and you are in danger."

Lyra stepped forward, her brow furrowed with confusion. "How did you get past the shadows?"

Cassian's heart raced, something about the entire situation making his skin crawl. He had always trusted Eryndor. The elder had been a guide to them, a mentor who had stood by their side during countless battles. But now, standing in the heart of the Citadel, something felt terribly wrong.

"I know the way through the darkness," Eryndor replied smoothly, his eyes flickering with an odd light. "I know the Citadel better than anyone."

Cassian exchanged a glance with his siblings, uneasy feeling gnawing at him. The Citadel had been under siege for hours—no one should have been able to slip through the shadows without being attacked. How had Eryndor gotten here so easily? Why did he seem so unaffected by the overwhelming presence of Tharion's magic?

Orion's grip on his sword tightened. "Why didn't you come sooner? We have been fighting for our lives out here."

Eryndor's eyes gleamed in the dim light, and he took a slow step forward, his voice soft but unnerving. "I was waiting for the right moment."

Lyra's breath hitched, her eyes widening in realization. "What... what are you saying?"

Cassian's heart sank as he looked into Eryndor's hollow gaze. His mind raced with the pieces falling into place—how the Citadel's defenses had fallen so easily, how Tharion had seemed to know their every move, how the fireflies' magic had been slowly drained, even before the attack had begun.

"You've been working with him," Cassian whispered, his voice barely audible.

Eryndor's lips curled into a cold, twisted smile. "I have done what was necessary."

Orion's eyes blazed with anger, and he stepped forward, his sword raised. "You betrayed us. You betrayed everything."

Eryndor's expression did not change. "Tharion's power is inevitable. The fireflies' light is weak, dying. I did what I had to do to survive."

Cassian's pulse raced, his mind reeling. This was not happening—Eryndor, the one who had taught them everything they knew about the Citadel, the fireflies, and their magic, had turned against them. The realization hit him like a hammer, and he struggled to keep his composure.

"Why?" Lyra's voice was a broken whisper. "Why would you do this?"

Eryndor's eyes darkened, and his voice dropped to a low, menacing tone. "Because you cannot fight the darkness forever. The fireflies' magic is fading, and soon, there will be nothing left but shadows. I have chosen the winning side."

Cassian felt a surge of anger and betrayal welling up inside him. "We trusted you. You have doomed the Citadel—doomed all of us."

Eryndor's smile widened, and for a moment, his face twisted into something almost inhuman. "The Citadel was doomed long before Tharion arrived. The fireflies were never strong enough to hold back the darkness."

Cassian's grip tightened on the crystal, his heart pounding in his chest. "We're not finished yet."

But before he could move, Eryndor raised his hand, and the shadows around him surged forward, coiling, and twisting toward the siblings like a wave of darkness. The crystal's light flickered weakly, barely enough to push the shadows back.

Orion swung his sword, but the shadows reformed almost instantly, swirling around them with terrifying speed. "He's feeding them—he's controlling the shadows!" Orion shouted.

Lyra's flute played a desperate, high-pitched melody, but the fireflies' light was faltering, their magic barely holding on. "Cassian! We have to stop him!"

Cassian's mind raced as the shadows closed in, Eryndor's twisted smile still haunting him. The fireflies' magic was slipping away, and now, the very person they had trusted to protect the Citadel had turned against them.

The darkness was overwhelming.

But they could not give up—not now.

"We stop him together," Cassian muttered, his voice filled with determination. "No matter what."

The siblings braced themselves for the battle ahead, their trust shattered, but their resolve unbroken. Eryndor had betrayed them, but they would not let the darkness win.

Chapter 28: Shattered Trust

The air in the chamber was thick with tension, the oppressive weight of betrayal hanging over the siblings like a suffocating fog. Master Eryndor's twisted smile lingered in the dim light of the crystal, his hollow eyes filled with a cold satisfaction. The shadows that coiled and writhed around him were no longer hidden—they moved at his command, responding to his every gesture like extensions of his will.

Cassian's heart pounded in his chest, his mind reeling from the revelation. The man they had trusted—the man who had guided them through the darkest days—had turned against them. Every warning, every lesson he had taught them, now felt like a cruel joke, a manipulation designed to lead them straight into Tharion's hands.

"You don't have to do this," Cassian said, his voice shaking with a mixture of anger and disbelief. "You can still stop this."

Eryndor's smile widened, his voice dripping with disdain. "You still do not understand, do you? This is already over. Tharion's power is greater than anything the fireflies could ever muster. The Citadel has fallen."

Orion stepped forward, his sword raised, his face contorted with rage. "You betrayed us," he snarled, his voice filled with venom. "You betrayed everything we stood for."

Eryndor's gaze flickered to Orion, and for a moment, something like pity crossed his face. "I did what was necessary. The fireflies were always too weak to stop the darkness. Tharion's power is the only way forward. I chose survival."

Lyra's breath hitched, her eyes wide with shock and hurt. "Survival?" she whispered, her voice trembling. "You chose to destroy everything. You let the shadows in."

Eryndor's expression hardened. "The shadows were always here, waiting. I simply opened the door."

Cassian felt a surge of anger and sorrow welling up inside him. "We trusted you," he muttered, his voice thick with emotion. "You were supposed to protect the Citadel. You were supposed to protect us."

Eryndor's eyes gleamed with a dim light. "I am protecting you. I am offering you a chance to stand with Tharion, to survive in the world that is coming."

Orion's jaw clenched as he took a step forward, his grip on his sword tightening. "We'd rather die fighting than stand with you."

The shadows around Eryndor rippled, swirling like a storm ready to break. "So be it."

Before Cassian could react, Eryndor raised his hand, and the shadows surged forward, faster, and more violently than before. The air filled with the sound of rushing wind, and the room grew darker as the tendrils of shadow reached out, clawing toward the siblings with a hunger that felt alive.

Orion swung his sword, slicing through the nearest tendril, but it reformed almost instantly, twisting, and curling around him like a snake. He grunted, struggling to free himself as the darkness tightened its grip.

"Lyra, now!" Cassian shouted, his voice filled with urgency.

Lyra's hands shook as she raised her flute to her lips, her face pale with fear. She played a sharp, high-pitched melody, the sound cutting through the air like a blade. The fireflies responded, their light flaring weakly as they pushed against the shadows, but Cassian could see it—it was not enough. Their magic was faltering, their light dimming with each passing second.

The shadows were too strong.

Cassian gripped the crystal, feeling its weak pulse in his hand. The fireflies' magic was still there, but it was slipping away, fading under the weight of Tharion's influence. They needed more power. They needed to reach the Heart.

"We have to get to the Heart," Cassian muttered, his voice barely audible over the sound of the battle. "It's the only way."

But Eryndor was not finished. He stepped forward, his eyes gleaming with malice as the shadows around him grew darker, thicker. "You will never reach the Heart," he hissed. "Tharion's power is absolute. You cannot stop him."

Orion slashed at another tendril of shadow, but his movements were slower now, his strength waning. "We'll stop you," he growled, his voice filled with defiance. "Even if it's the last thing we do."

Cassian's mind raced as he looked at the crystal, the faint light flickering weakly in his hand. The fireflies' magic was their only hope, but it was not enough. Not like this.

There had to be another way.

Suddenly, a thought struck him—a desperate, reckless thought, but it was the only chance they had. The fireflies' magic was fading because it was being drained by the shadows. But what if they could reverse it? What if they could tap into the Heart's remaining power and use it to amplify the fireflies' light?

"Lyra," Cassian gasped, his voice filled with urgency. "Play the melody again, but this time... draw the magic from the Heart."

Lyra's eyes widened in surprise. "What? I do not know if I can—"

"You can," Cassian interrupted, his voice firm. "The fireflies' magic is connected to the Heart. If we can tap into that power, we might have a chance."

Lyra hesitated for a moment, her hands trembling as she raised her flute again. "I'll try," she whispered, her voice shaky but determined.

As Lyra began to play, the melody shifted, taking on a deeper, more haunting tone. The sound resonated through the chamber, vibrating in the very air, and for a moment, Cassian could feel it—the pulse of the Heart, faint but growing stronger with each note.

The crystal in his hand glowed brighter, and the fireflies' light flared, pushing back the shadows with renewed strength. The tendrils that had wrapped around Orion loosened, dissolving into mist as the light grew stronger.

Eryndor's eyes widened in surprise, his expression twisting with anger. "No... this cannot be."

But Cassian was not finished. He stepped forward, the crystal blazing in his hand as the fireflies' magic surged through him. "You underestimated us, Eryndor. You underestimated the fireflies."

With a roar of determination, Cassian raised the crystal high, its light flooding the chamber with a brilliant glow. The shadows recoiled, hissing as they were driven back, their dark forms shrinking under the force of the fireflies' magic.

Eryndor stumbled back, his face contorted with rage and fear. "This isn't over," he spat, his voice trembling with fury. "Tharion's power will consume you."

But Cassian's eyes blazed with determination. "Not today."

With one final burst of energy, the fireflies' light exploded outward, filling the chamber with a blinding flash of brilliance. The shadows dissolved, and Eryndor's twisted form was thrown back, disappearing into the darkness with a scream of rage.

The chamber fell silent, the only sound the faint hum of the fireflies' magic as it settled, its light flickering but steady.

Cassian lowered the crystal, his breath coming in ragged gasps as he looked at his siblings. "We're not done yet," he said, his voice filled with determination. "We still have to reach the Heart."

Orion nodded, his face pale but resolute. "Let's finish this."

Chapter 29: Into the Depths

The light from the fireflies cast a faint, flickering glow across the crumbling stone walls as Cassian, Lyra, and Orion made their way deeper into the Heart of the Citadel. Every step felt heavier than the last, as though the weight of the shadows clinging to the air was trying to drag them back. The sound of their breathing echoed softly in the vast, cavernous space, broken only by the occasional distant rumble as the Citadel groaned under the strain of Tharion's dark magic.

The confrontation with Eryndor had left a bitter taste in Cassian's mouth, but there was no time to dwell on it now. They were closer than ever to the source of the fireflies' power—closer to the last hope they had of stopping Tharion. The crystal in his hand pulsed weakly, its light dim but steady. He could feel the fireflies' magic flowing through it, but it was strained, as though fighting against the overwhelming presence of darkness that seeped through the walls of the Citadel.

"We need to move quickly," Cassian muttered, his voice tense. "The Heart won't hold much longer."

Lyra's face was pale, her eyes wide with a mixture of fear and determination. She clutched her flute tightly, her fingers trembling as they walked. "I can still feel it... the fireflies' magic. It is there, but it is fading."

Orion grunted in agreement, his sword gleaming faintly in the fireflies' glow. "We are close. We have to be."

The corridor ahead opened into a massive chamber—far larger than any they had seen before. The Heart of the Citadel stood at the center, a towering structure of ancient stone, covered in intricate runes that pulsed faintly with light. But the sight that greeted them sent a chill down Cassian's spine.

The Heart was not as they had hoped. Black tendrils of shadow wrapped around its base, twisting, and writhing like living things, seeping into the stone, and corrupting the once-brilliant magic that had protected the Citadel for generations. The air in the chamber was thick with the stench of decay, and the shadows that clung to the walls seemed to ripple with malevolent intent.

Cassian swallowed hard, his grip tightening on the crystal. "Tharion's already reached it..."

Orion's jaw clenched as he stepped forward, his sword raised. "We cannot let him destroy it. If the Heart falls, the fireflies' magic dies with it."

Lyra's hands trembled as she raised her flute, her eyes locked on the Heart. "We need to cleanse it," she whispered, her voice filled with fear. "But the corruption... it's too strong."

Cassian's mind raced as he looked at the Heart, the dark tendrils pulsating with Tharion's power. The fireflies' light was still there, but it was weak buried beneath the layers of darkness that had wrapped themselves around it like a suffocating blanket.

"We don't have much time," he said, his voice filled with urgency. "We have to find a way to break the corruption."

Before they could move, a low, deep rumble filled the chamber, and the air seemed to grow colder, heavier. Cassian's heart pounded in his chest as he looked around, his pulse quickening with dread.

From the shadows at the far end of the chamber, a figure began to emerge—tall, cloaked in darkness, his form shifting and twisting like smoke.

Tharion.

His presence filled the room, his eyes glowing with a malevolent light that seemed to drain the very air of warmth. The shadows rippled around him, responding to his every movement like an extension of his will. He stepped forward slowly, his voice a low, mocking growl.

"You've come so far, children of Evelyn," Tharion said, his voice filled with cruel amusement. "But it ends here."

Cassian's breath caught in his throat as the full weight of Tharion's presence pressed down on them. The air grew thick with malice, and the shadows around the Heart pulsed with renewed strength, feeding off the dark energy that radiated from him.

Lyra's hands shook as she raised her flute, her voice trembling. "We... we have to stop him..."

Orion stepped forward, his sword gleaming in the faint light of the crystal. "We're not afraid of you, Tharion."

Tharion's lips curled into a cruel smile, and the shadows around him seemed to grow darker, more twisted. "You should be."

Without warning, Tharion raised his hand, and the shadows surged forward, faster, and more violently than before. The tendrils of darkness lashed out, wrapping around the Heart, choking the fireflies' light, and sending a wave of corruption through the chamber.

Cassian gasped as the crystal in his hand flickered, its light sputtering as the shadows closed in. He could feel the fireflies' magic slipping away, struggling against the overwhelming power of Tharion's dark influence.

"We need to push him back," Cassian shouted, his voice filled with desperation. "We can't let him take the Heart!"

Orion charged forward, his sword slicing through the nearest tendrils of shadow, but they reformed almost instantly, their dark forms growing stronger with each second. Lyra's flute played a frantic melody, but the fireflies' light was faltering, barely enough to keep the shadows at bay.

"We can't hold them off!" Lyra cried, her voice filled with panic. "Tharion's too strong!"

Cassian's mind raced as he looked at the Heart, the corruption spreading faster than they could fight it. The fireflies' magic was slipping away, and the shadows were growing too powerful.

But they could not give up. Not now.

With a surge of determination, Cassian raised the crystal high, its light flaring weakly in his hand. "We need to reach the Heart!" he shouted. "We need to use its power!"

Orion gritted his teeth, his face twisted with effort as he fought back the shadows. "Then we move—now."

Together, the siblings pushed forward, their movements slow and labored under the weight of the darkness that filled the chamber. The shadows lashed out at them, clawing, and twisting around their limbs, but they pressed on, their eyes locked on the Heart.

Cassian could feel the fireflies' magic pulsing through the crystal, weak but still there, still fighting. "We're almost there," he muttered through gritted teeth. "We just need to—"

Before he could finish, the ground beneath them shook violently, and a deafening crack echoed through the chamber. The Heart shuddered, its ancient stone groaning under the strain of the dark magic that surrounded it.

Cassian's heart leapt into his throat as he saw it—the Heart was breaking.

"We're out of time," Lyra gasped, her voice filled with terror. "It's collapsing!"

Tharion's laughter filled the chamber, cold and mocking. "You cannot stop what is already in motion. The fireflies' magic is finished."

The Heart trembled again, the cracks spreading further as the shadows coiled tighter around it, feeding off its magic. The fireflies' light flickered weakly, their power slipping away with each passing second.

Cassian's pulse quickened, his mind racing. We are so close... we cannot fail now.

With a roar of determination, he raised the crystal high, its light flaring brighter than before. "We won't let you destroy everything!" he shouted, his voice filled with desperation.

Tharion's eyes blazed with fury as he raised his hand, and the shadows surged forward in one final, crushing wave.

Cassian braced himself, the fireflies' magic surging through him as the darkness closed in around them. This was it—their last chance.

They could not fail.

Chapter 30: The Breaking Point

The ground shook beneath their feet, the ancient stone of the Citadel groaning as the Heart of the Citadel began to collapse. Dark cracks spread like jagged veins through the once-sacred structure, and the fireflies' light flickered weakly, barely holding on. The air was thick with corruption, the shadows swirling violently around them, growing darker and more aggressive with every passing second.

Cassian's heart raced as he clutched the crystal in his hand, its light pulsing faintly. The fireflies' magic was slipping away fading under the relentless pressure of Tharion's dark influence. He could feel the weight of the shadows pressing down on him, cold and suffocating, like a heavy shroud pulling him toward the abyss.

"We're out of time," Orion grunted, his voice strained as he fought back the tendrils of shadow that lashed at them from all sides. His sword gleamed in the faint light, but every strike felt slower, weaker, as the darkness pressed in. "The Heart's going to fall."

Lyra's face was pale, her breath coming in shallow gasps as she played her flute, trying to hold the fireflies' light steady. "I cannot... I cannot keep them back," she whispered, her voice trembling with fear. "Tharion's too strong."

Cassian's pulse quickened as he glanced toward the Heart, the corruption spreading faster than they could contain it. Black tendrils of shadow wrapped around the ancient structure, tightening their grip with every second, suffocating the fireflies' magic. The cracks in the stone were growing deeper, wider—the very foundation of the Citadel was crumbling.

"We have to do something," Cassian muttered through gritted teeth, his mind racing. "We can't let him destroy the Heart."

Tharion's cold laughter echoed through the chamber, deep and mocking, sending chills down Cassian's spine. The ancient sorcerer stood at the far end of the room, his form shifting and twisting like a living shadow. His eyes gleamed with a malevolent light, filled with dark triumph.

"You still believe you can stop me?" Tharion's voice was a low growl, filled with cruel amusement. "This is the end, children. The fireflies' magic is finished. The Citadel will fall, and with it, all your hopes."

Cassian's breath caught in his throat as the full weight of Tharion's words pressed down on him. His hands trembled as he looked at the crystal in his grasp, its light flickering weakly. The fireflies' power was slipping away, and the Heart was on the verge of collapse.

We are so close... we cannot fail now.

"We won't give up," Cassian muttered, his voice filled with determination. "We won't let you win."

Orion swung his sword in a wide arc, slicing through the nearest tendril of shadow, but his movements were slower than before, his strength fading under the relentless assault of the darkness. "We can't hold them off much longer," he grunted, his voice filled with strain. "Cassian, we need a plan. Now."

Cassian's mind raced as he looked at the Heart, the dark tendrils tightening their grip with every second. The fireflies' light was still weak, but still burning. If they could find a way to break the corruption, even for a moment, maybe the fireflies' magic could regain its strength.

"We need to break Tharion's hold on the Heart," Cassian said, his voice filled with urgency. "If we can cut off the corruption, even for a second, the fireflies might be able to push him back."

Lyra's hands trembled as she lowered her flute, her face pale with exhaustion. "But how? The shadows are everywhere. We cannot even get close."

Cassian's grip tightened on the crystal, his mind spinning. The fireflies' magic was tied to the Heart, and the crystal was their only connection to that power. But the shadows were feeding on it—draining the light with every second. If they could sever that connection, even briefly, they might stand a chance.

"We need to overload the crystal," Cassian muttered, his voice barely audible. "Use the last of the fireflies' magic to break the corruption."

Orion's eyes widened in shock. "Overload it? Are you crazy? That could destroy the Heart—and us with it."

Cassian swallowed hard, his heart pounding in his chest. "It is a risk we have to take. If we do not do something now, the Heart will fall, and there will not be anything left to save."

Lyra's breath hitched, her eyes wide with fear. "But what if we fail? What if the crystal cannot hold it?"

Cassian looked at his siblings, his chest tight with the weight of the decision. The fireflies' magic was their only hope, but if they did not act, the shadows would consume everything. They could not hold out much longer.

"We have to try," he said, his voice firm. "It's our only chance."

Orion gritted his teeth, his face lined with tension. "Then let's do it."

Lyra nodded shakily, raising her flute once more. "I'll do my best," she whispered, her voice filled with determination.

Cassian took a deep breath, focusing all his energy on the crystal in his hand. The fireflies' magic pulsed weakly within it, but he could still feel it—their connection to the Heart, to the light that had protected the Citadel for so long.

"Together," Cassian muttered, his voice filled with resolve. "We do this together."

With a sharp intake of breath, Cassian channeled the fireflies' magic into the crystal, pushing it beyond its limits. The light flared, brighter than before, filling the chamber with a brilliant glow that pushed back the shadows, if only for a moment.

Lyra's melody filled the air, deep and haunting, resonating with the ancient magic of the Heart. The fireflies responded, their light surging as they fought against the corruption, their magic flaring brighter with every note.

Tharion's expression twisted with fury as he raised his hand, sending a wave of dark energy crashing toward them. The shadows lashed out violently, their tendrils writhing and twisting as they tried to smother the fireflies' light.

But Cassian held on, his grip on the crystal tightening as the light flared brighter, pushing back the darkness. He could feel the fireflies' magic surging through him, stronger than before—fighting back, resisting Tharion's hold.

"We're doing it," Cassian gasped, his voice filled with hope. "We're breaking through."

But just as the fireflies' light reached its peak, a deafening crack echoed through the chamber, and the ground beneath them shuddered violently. The Heart of the Citadel trembled, its ancient stone groaning under the strain of the battle.

Cassian's breath caught in his throat as he saw it—the cracks in the Heart were deepening, spreading further, faster. The fireflies' magic was growing stronger, but the Heart itself was falling apart.

"We're too late," Lyra whispered, her voice filled with terror. "The Heart... it's breaking."

Tharion's laughter filled the chamber, cold and triumphant. "You cannot save it. The fireflies' magic is doomed."

Cassian's pulse quickened, his mind racing. They were so close, but the Heart could not hold much longer. The fireflies' light was growing stronger, but the foundation of the Citadel was collapsing.

"We need to push harder," Orion growled, his voice filled with desperation. "We can't stop now."

Cassian nodded, his heart pounding. "One last push."

Together, the siblings poured everything they had into the crystal, the fireflies' light blazing brighter than it ever had before. The shadows recoiled, hissing, and writhing as the light pierced through the darkness, driving them back.

But the Heart... the Heart was breaking.

With a final, blinding flash of light, the fireflies' magic surged forward, and the chamber was consumed by brilliance.

And then, the Heart shattered.

Chapter 31: Shattered Light

For a moment, everything was silent. The brilliance of the fireflies' magic had consumed the chamber, blinding and all-encompassing. Cassian could hear nothing but the ringing in his ears, his breath shallow as he tried to steady himself. His body felt weightless, suspended in the glow of the fireflies' final surge. Then, all at once, the light vanished, leaving a cold, suffocating darkness in its wake.

Cassian hit the ground hard, the impact jarring him back to reality. The stone beneath him was cold, rough, and covered in debris. His limbs ached, and his chest heaved as he gasped for air. The overwhelming silence was broken only by the faint sound of crumbling stone and distant echoes.

"Orion? Lyra?" Cassian croaked, his voice weak and hoarse. Panic surged through him as he blinked into the darkness, trying to find his siblings.

There was a groan from nearby, and Cassian's heart leapt with relief. He crawled toward the sound, his fingers scraping across the stone until he reached Orion, who was struggling to sit up. Orion's face was pale, his breathing labored, but he was alive.

"I'm... here," Orion grunted, wincing as he clutched his side. "What... happened?"

Cassian swallowed hard, his gaze sweeping the ruined chamber. The Heart of the Citadel lay in pieces—large chunks of stone scattered across the floor, its once-glowing runes now dull and lifeless. The fireflies' magic, which had once filled the room with warmth and light, was gone.

"We... we broke the Heart," Cassian whispered, his voice hollow.

Orion's eyes widened as he followed Cassian's gaze, his expression darkening with realization. "The fireflies... their magic..."

Cassian's chest tightened. The Heart had been their last hope. They had poured everything they had into the fireflies' light, but in the end, the Heart had shattered under the weight of Tharion's corruption.

A faint, trembling voice cut through the silence. "Cassian..."

Cassian's heart leapt as he turned toward the sound. Lyra was slumped against a broken pillar, her flute lying on the ground beside her. Her face was streaked with dirt, and her body shook with exhaustion, but she was alive.

"Lyra!" Cassian rushed to her side, his hands trembling as he helped her sit up. "Are you all, right?"

Lyra's breath came in short, ragged bursts as she nodded weakly. "I... I think so," she whispered, though her voice was barely audible. "The fireflies... I felt their light... but now..."

Cassian's throat tightened as he glanced at the shattered Heart. "The Heart is gone," he muttered, his voice thick with guilt. "We tried, but it wasn't enough."

Orion limped over to join them, his face grim. "So, what now?" he asked, his voice low. "The fireflies' magic is gone, the Heart is destroyed... and Tharion is still out there."

Cassian clenched his fists, his pulse racing. They had fought so hard, come so far, but now... now they were standing in the ruins of everything they had tried to protect. The weight of failure pressed down on him like a crushing tide.

"I don't know," Cassian admitted, his voice filled with despair. "I don't know how we can stop him now."

But before anyone could respond, the air in the chamber shifted. A low, cold laugh echoed through the darkness—deep and mocking, sending chills down Cassian's spine.

"Did you really believe you could win?"

Cassian's blood ran cold as Tharion's voice filled the room, his presence suffocating. The shadows began to stir, rippling like a black tide as they spread across the floor, creeping toward the siblings with deadly intent. Tharion's form materialized from the darkness, his eyes glowing with malevolent light.

"You fought so hard," Tharion sneered, his voice dripping with cruelty. "But in the end, you only hastened your own destruction."

Orion stepped forward, his sword raised, though his movements were sluggish, weakened by the battle. "We're not finished yet," he growled, his voice filled with defiance.

Tharion's laughter echoed through the chamber like a death knell. "Oh, but you are," he hissed. "The Heart is broken. The fireflies' magic is gone. And now, the Citadel will fall."

Cassian's heart pounded in his chest as the shadows closed in, their dark forms slithering and writhing like living creatures. The air grew colder, heavier, as though the very life of the Citadel was being drained away.

"We have to do something," Lyra gasped, her voice filled with panic. "We can't let him destroy everything."

But Cassian's mind was blank. The crystal in his hand, once a beacon of light, was now cold and lifeless. The fireflies' magic had faded, and with it, their hope of stopping Tharion. What can we do?

Tharion's eyes gleamed with triumph as he stepped closer, his dark power radiating from him like a suffocating aura. "You are nothing without the fireflies," he said, his voice low and filled with malice. "And now, you will die with them."

Cassian's breath hitched in his throat as the shadows closed in, their tendrils reaching out to wrap around him, cold and relentless. He felt the weight of the darkness pressing against his skin, seeping into his bones, pulling him down into the abyss.

But just as the last flicker of hope began to fade, a faint light pulsed in the distance—weak, but present.

Cassian's eyes widened in shock as he turned toward the source of the light. Deep within the shattered remains of the Heart, something was glowing faint, but unmistakable. The fireflies' magic had not disappeared completely.

"There!" Cassian shouted, his voice filled with urgency. "The fireflies' magic—it's still there!"

Orion and Lyra turned to look, their eyes widening with disbelief. The glow was faint, barely more than a flicker, but it was real.

Tharion's expression twisted with fury as he followed their gaze. "No... that's impossible."

Cassian's pulse quickened, his heart racing with a renewed sense of hope. "We're not finished yet," he muttered, his voice filled with determination.

With a surge of energy, Cassian scrambled toward the shattered Heart, his body aching with every step. The shadows lashed out at him, clawing, and twisting around his limbs, but he pushed forward, his eyes locked on the faint glow of the fireflies' magic.

"We have to protect the light," Lyra shouted, raising her flute as she played a sharp, haunting melody. The fireflies responded, their weak light flickering as they gathered around her, pushing back the shadows.

Orion stood beside her, his sword gleaming in the faint light as he slashed through the tendrils of shadow that lashed out at them. "We hold them off," he growled, his voice filled with determination. "Cassian, get to the Heart."

Cassian nodded, his breath coming in ragged gasps as he reached the shattered remains of the Heart. The glow was coming from deep within the cracks, a faint, pulsing light that seemed to call to him.

The fireflies' magic... It is still alive.

With trembling hands, Cassian reached into the cracks, his fingers brushing against the source of the light. The moment he touched it, a surge of energy rushed through him—weak, but filled with warmth and life. The fireflies' magic was not gone—it was hidden, buried deep within the ruins of the Heart.

"We can still save it," Cassian muttered, his voice filled with hope. "We can still save the fireflies."

But as the light flared, Tharion's eyes blazed with fury. "You will not defy me!"

With a roar of rage, Tharion raised his hand, and the shadows surged forward in a violent wave, crashing toward the siblings with deadly force.

Cassian's heart pounded in his chest as he clutched the fireflies' light, his mind racing. This is it.

They could not fail now.

Chapter 32: The Vault's Secret

As the shadows pressed closer, swirling violently around the shattered Heart of the Citadel, Lyra's hands trembled on her flute. The fireflies' magic was flickering, barely holding on, and despite their desperate attempts, it felt like they were on the verge of losing everything. Tharion's laughter echoed through the chamber, dark and mocking, filling the air with a suffocating weight.

"We're running out of time," Orion growled through clenched teeth as he slashed at the dark tendrils lashing toward them. "Cassian, we need that light now!"

Cassian struggled to channel the faint energy pulsing from the shattered Heart, his body straining against the overwhelming force of the shadows. But even as he reached for the fireflies' magic, it was not enough. Tharion's influence was too strong, too all-encompassing.

Lyra's mind raced, fear gripping her heart as the battle grew more desperate. And then, like a whisper from the past, her mother's voice echoed in her memory—a soft, reassuring voice filled with warmth.

"If the fireflies' magic ever falters, there is a way to restore it. The scroll... hidden in the Citadel's vault. Remember the poem, Lyra. It holds the key."

Lyra's breath hitched as the memory crashed into her. The scroll—her mother had told her about it long ago when she was still a child. She had dismissed it as an old story, a tale passed down from generation to generation. But now, in the midst of the darkness, she realized it was not just a story. The scroll was real, and it held the secret to saving the fireflies.

"There's a way," Lyra whispered, her voice trembling. "There is a scroll... locked in the Citadel's vault. My mother told me about it. It holds a poem that can help restore the fireflies' magic."

Cassian's head snapped toward her, his eyes wide with shock. "A scroll? Why didn't you say something earlier?"

"I—I forgot," Lyra stammered, guilt flashing across her face. "It was so long ago. I did not realize it was real until now."

Orion cursed under his breath, his eyes flicking between the advancing shadows and his siblings. "Where is this vault? Can we reach it?"

Lyra swallowed hard, her mind racing as she recalled her mother's words. "The vault is deep in the Citadel, hidden beneath the main chamber. It is protected by powerful wards... but if we can get to it, the scroll should be inside."

Cassian's pulse quickened as hope surged through him. "Then we need to move—now."

"But the shadows," Lyra protested, her voice filled with doubt. "Tharion is everywhere. He will not let us reach the vault."

Orion's eyes gleamed with determination as he raised his sword. "We'll make a path."

Tharion's laughter grew louder, his form shifting and twisting in the darkness. "You think you can escape?" he sneered. "There is nowhere to run. The fireflies' magic is mine, and soon, the Citadel will fall."

Cassian's heart pounded in his chest, but he refused to back down. "We are not running. We are going to stop you."

With a nod to his siblings, Cassian led the charge, his heart racing as they pushed through the swirling shadows, their destination clear—the vault. Every step felt like a battle, the shadows clawing at them, trying to drag them down, but they pressed on, driven by the hope that the scroll would hold the key to saving everything.

The journey through the Citadel's ruined halls was grueling. The walls groaned under the weight of the dark magic that had seeped into every crack and corner, and the floor beneath them trembled with each step they took. Cassian's grip on the crystal tightened as the fireflies' faint light guided them forward, but it was dimming—fading with every second they wasted.

"We're almost there," Lyra muttered, her voice tight with fear. "The vault is just ahead."

As they rounded a corner, a massive stone door loomed before them, its surface covered in ancient runes that glowed faintly with protective wards. The door to the vault. Cassian's breath caught in his throat as he saw it—this was the last barrier between them and the scroll.

Orion stepped forward, his sword raised, his eyes scanning the door. "How do we open it?"

Lyra's brow furrowed as she studied the runes, her mind racing. "The wards... they are ancient. We need to use the fireflies' magic to break through. My mother said the scroll is tied to their light."

Cassian nodded, his heart pounding as he held up the crystal. The fireflies' magic was weak, but it was still there—still fighting. "I'll try."

With a deep breath, Cassian pressed the crystal against the door, willing the fireflies' magic to surge through him. For a moment, nothing happened. The runes remained still, lifeless, and Cassian's heart sank.

But then, slowly, the runes began to glow brighter, pulsing in time with the fireflies' light. The door shuddered, the wards flickering as the ancient magic began to respond.

"We're doing it," Cassian muttered, his voice filled with hope.

But just as the door began to open, a deafening roar echoed through the hall, and the shadows surged forward with renewed fury. Tharion's voice filled the air, cold and filled with rage. "You will not escape!"

The shadows lashed out violently, crashing toward them like a black tidal wave.

"Orion!" Cassian shouted, his voice filled with urgency.

Orion stepped in front of his siblings, his sword gleaming in the fireflies' light as he slashed through the nearest tendrils of shadow. "I've got this—just get that door open!"

Lyra's hands shook as she raised her flute, playing a soft, desperate melody that resonated with the fireflies' magic. The light flared, pushing back the Shadows just enough to give Cassian time.

With one final push, the door to the vault creaked open, revealing a dark chamber beyond. At the center of the room, resting on a pedestal, was an ancient scroll—its surface covered in golden, glowing symbols.

"The scroll," Lyra gasped, her eyes wide with awe.

Cassian's heart raced as he stepped toward it. "This is it... this is how we save the fireflies."

But as they reached for the scroll, the shadows surged again, more violent than before. Tharion was not finished yet.

Chapter 33: The Words of Power

C assian's hands trembled as he reached for the scroll, its ancient surface glowing faintly beneath his fingers. The golden symbols on the parchment pulsed in rhythm with the fading fireflies' light, as if the very magic of the Citadel were waiting for him to read the words aloud.

The shadows twisted violently around them, Tharion's dark magic suffocating the air. His voice, deep and filled with venom, echoed through the chamber. "You cannot stop what is already in motion. The fireflies are mine. The Citadel will fall, and your light will be snuffed out."

Lyra and Orion stood close by, their faces pale but determined. The weight of their mother's memory pressed down on them, and Lyra's eyes flickered with something deeper—a realization. Cassian knew she remembered what their mother had told her about the scroll and the poem that could save the fireflies.

"This is it," Lyra whispered, her voice trembling as she looked at the scroll. "The poem... it holds the key."

Cassian's heart pounded as he unrolled the scroll, revealing the words written in a language older than the Citadel itself. The fireflies' light, weak and flickering, responded to the scroll's presence, glowing faintly as the magic within the words began to awaken.

"These words," Cassian muttered, his voice filled with awe. "They are not just a poem. They are alive with the fireflies' magic."

He scanned the lines, his breath catching as he read the familiar words—words that seemed to come from a distant memory, as if he had heard them long ago.

Lyra's voice wavered as she stood beside him, her eyes wide with recognition. "It's our mother's poem," she whispered. "She told us this story when we were children..."

Cassian nodded, his throat tight with emotion. The poem was more than just words. It was a spell—an incantation that could reignite the fireflies' light. But the power within it was fragile, and he knew they had to be careful.

Orion, his sword still raised, glanced toward the entrance of the vault where the shadows swirled, threatening to consume them. "We don't have time to be careful," he said, his voice sharp. "If this poem can save the fireflies, you need to read it—now."

With trembling hands, Cassian began to recite the poem, his voice steady but filled with urgency. As the words slipped from his lips, the fireflies responded, their light growing stronger, pushing back the darkness inch by inch. The ancient magic within the scroll flared to life, and the poem, Fireflies of the Heart, took hold.

"In midnight's chill, where shadows creep,
I hear the whispers of hearts asleep.
Through the fog, the fireflies glow,
Flickering lights from long ago."

The fireflies, once fading and weak, flared to life as Cassian's voice filled the chamber. Their light brightened, casting a warm, golden glow across the vault. The shadows recoiled, hissing as the fireflies' magic surged.

Tharion's furious presence grew stronger, his voice a cold snarl. "No! You cannot revive them!"

But Cassian pressed on, his voice growing stronger as the magic of the poem flowed through him. Each line seemed to echo through time, carrying with it the power of the fireflies and the love they had once protected.

"Ghostly embers, soft and pale,
Their silent dance begins the tale.
A love once bright, now faint, decayed,
Trapped in the dark where memories fade."

Lyra's flute echoed softly, her melody weaving through the words of the poem, guiding the fireflies' light as it pushed back against Tharion's dark magic. The siblings could feel it—the fireflies' magic growing stronger, their light burning brighter.

Orion fought at the edge of the vault, his sword gleaming in the fireflies' glow as he cut through the encroaching shadows. "Keep going!" he shouted, his voice filled with determination. "It's working!"

Cassian's heart raced as he continued to recite the poem, his voice filled with the weight of their mother's legacy.

"Their glow, a breath from distant time,
Flickers in rhythm, a ghostly rhyme.
Each pulse a heart that dared to feel,
Now bound in shadows, cold as steel."

The fireflies pulsed in time with his words, their light pushing back the cold darkness that surrounded them. The shadows that had once suffocated the Citadel were breaking, weakening under the weight of the poem's magic.

Tharion's roar of anger echoed through the chamber, but Cassian could sense the shift. The fireflies were winning—slowly, but surely.

"They flutter through the hollow night,
Lost in the veil, beyond the light.
A spark of love that once burned bright,
Now fades to whispers, out of sight."

The ground beneath them trembled as the fireflies' light flared, filling the vault with brilliant, golden radiance. The poem had unlocked something deep within the fireflies, a power they had not known they possessed—a power that could defeat the darkness.

Cassian's breath caught as he reached the final verses, his voice trembling with emotion.

"But in the dark, they never die,
These fireflies of the heart still fly.
In every pulse, in every gleam,
They haunt the edges of a dream."

As the last words of the poem left his lips, the fireflies' light exploded outward, flooding the Citadel with brilliance. The darkness recoiled violently, Tharion's furious scream echoing through the chamber as his power was overwhelmed by the fireflies' magic.

For after a moment, the shadows were gone. The air was filled with the warm, comforting glow of the fireflies, their magic restored, their light blazing brighter than ever before.

"We did it," Lyra whispered, her eyes filled with awe. "The fireflies... they're saved."

But as the siblings stood in the golden glow of the fireflies, Cassian's heart tightened. Tharion had been driven back, but they all knew he was not defeated. The fireflies had been restored, but the battle was far from over.

And the final confrontation was drawing near.

Chapter 34: The Final Reckoning

The warm glow of the fireflies filled the vault, their light pulsing with renewed strength. Cassian, Lyra, and Orion stood in the heart of the Citadel, surrounded by the golden brilliance that had once seemed lost forever. The air was no longer suffocating with darkness, but there was an unsettling stillness—a calm before the storm.

Cassian's breath came in shallow gasps as he lowered the scroll, his heart pounding from the weight of what they had just accomplished. The fireflies' magic had been restored, their light blazing bright once more, but deep in his chest, Cassian knew this victory was fleeting. Tharion was not gone—his presence lingered in the very walls of the Citadel, his rage festering like a wound.

Lyra's flute hung loosely in her hand as she looked around, her eyes wide with wonder. "We did it," she whispered, her voice soft with disbelief. "We saved the fireflies."

Orion wiped the sweat from his brow, his sword still raised as he scanned the vault for any sign of movement. "It's not over yet," he said grimly. "Tharion will not let this go. He will come at us harder than before."

Cassian nodded, his throat tight with tension. "He is weakened, but he is still out there. And he will not stop until the fireflies are gone."

The fireflies swirled around them, their light dancing in the air like a thousand tiny embers. Cassian felt their magic thrumming through the walls of the Citadel, stronger now, but still fragile. Tharion's corruption had left deep scars on the Citadel, and even with the fireflies' power restored, the battle was far from won.

"We need to be ready," Lyra said, her voice steady despite the fear in her eyes. "Tharion's going to come after us, and this time, he won't hold anything back."

Cassian clenched his fists, the memory of the poem still fresh in his mind. Their mother's words had given them hope, but it was up to them to finish what she had started. Tharion had nearly destroyed the Citadel, but the fireflies had survived, and as long as they held the light, they had a chance.

Suddenly, a deep, echoing rumble shook the walls of the Citadel, and the air grew thick with an overwhelming sense of dread. The warmth of the fireflies' light dimmed slightly as if their power was being smothered by a force far greater than before.

Cassian's heart leaped into his throat as he turned toward the entrance of the vault. "He's coming."

Orion's grip on his sword tightened as the shadows outside the vault began to twist and writhe, coiling like serpents ready to strike. "Get ready," he muttered, his voice low but filled with determination. "This is it."

Lyra stepped beside Cassian, her flute raised to her lips as she prepared to summon the fireflies' light once more. Her eyes met his, and Cassian could see the fear behind her steady gaze, but he also saw the same resolve that had kept them fighting.

"We won't let him take the fireflies," she whispered, her voice trembling with determination.

Cassian nodded, his pulse quickening as the shadows at the entrance of the vault began to shift. The air grew colder, and a dark, malevolent presence filled the chamber. Tharion was here.

The shadows parted, revealing the towering form of the ancient sorcerer, his body cloaked in darkness. His eyes, burning with rage, fixed on the siblings with a hatred that seemed to radiate through the room. The very air around him crackled with dark energy, his presence suffocating, as if the darkness itself bent to his will.

"You think you can stop me?" Tharion hissed, his voice low and filled with venom. "You are children playing with forces you do not understand."

Orion stepped forward, his sword gleaming in the faint light of the fireflies. "We understand more than you think," he growled, his voice steady. "We've fought you before, and we'll do it again."

Tharion's lips twisted into a cruel smile, and the shadows around him seemed to pulse with dark power. "You are fools," he sneered. "The fireflies' light may have been restored, but it is fleeting. Their magic is fragile, and I will see it snuffed out—along with your pathetic lives."

Cassian felt the weight of Tharion's words pressing down on him, but he refused to let fear take hold. He could feel the fireflies' magic coursing through him, their light a beacon of hope in the overwhelming darkness. He knew they had one last chance to stop Tharion, but it would take everything they had.

With a deep breath, Cassian raised the crystal that held the fireflies' light, his grip tightening as the magic within it flared to life. "We're not afraid of you," he said, his voice firm. "We have the fireflies' magic, and we'll use it to defeat you."

Tharion's eyes gleamed with fury as he raised his hand, and the shadows surged forward, lashing out like black tendrils toward the siblings. The air around them grew thick with dark magic, the force of Tharion's power suffocating.

"Now!" Cassian shouted, his voice filled with urgency.

Lyra raised her flute, her melody sharp and clear as it filled the chamber, the sound weaving through the air like a beacon of light. The fireflies responded instantly, their golden glow flaring to life, pushing back the shadows as their light surged.

Orion swung his sword with deadly precision, cutting through the nearest tendrils of shadow as they lashed toward him. His movements were quick and fierce, every strike fueled by the fireflies' magic.

Tharion roared in anger as the fireflies' light pierced through the darkness, weakening his grip on the Citadel. But even as the light surged, Cassian could feel the strain—it was taking everything they had to keep Tharion at bay.

"We need more power," Cassian muttered through gritted teeth, his voice strained. "The fireflies can't hold him off for long."

Lyra's melody wavered for a moment, her face pale with exhaustion, but she kept playing, her notes pushing the fireflies' light forward, forcing the shadows back inch by inch.

Tharion's voice boomed through the chamber, filled with rage. "You cannot win! I am the darkness, and the fireflies' light is nothing against me!"

Cassian's heart pounded in his chest as he clutched the crystal tighter. The fireflies' magic was strong, but Tharion's power was ancient and relentless. The darkness seemed to close in from all sides, suffocating and overpowering the fragile light.

But then, a memory flashed through Cassian's mind—a memory of their mother's voice, soft and reassuring, from a time long ago.

"The fireflies never die, Cassian. Even in the darkest night, their light will always find a way."

Cassian's breath caught in his throat, his pulse quickening as he realized what he had to do. The fireflies' magic was more than just a source of power—it was a living force, a connection to the hearts that had once protected the Citadel. They needed to give themselves to the fireflies, to become one with their light.

"We can do this," Cassian whispered, his voice filled with a quiet certainty. "We just need to trust the fireflies. Let their light guide us."

Lyra's eyes met his, and for a moment, she seemed to understand. She nodded, her melody shifting into something deeper, more haunting—a melody that resonated with the fireflies' light, calling to them, asking them to rise once more.

As the music filled the air, Cassian closed his eyes, allowing the fireflies' magic to flow through him. The crystal in his hand pulsed with life, and he felt the fireflies respond, their light flaring brighter, stronger. The darkness around them trembled, weakening under the weight of the fireflies' magic.

Orion's sword gleamed with a golden glow as the fireflies' light flowed through him, his strikes faster, more powerful. Together, the siblings stood united, their hearts and souls bound to the fireflies, their light surging in a final push against Tharion's dark magic.

The shadows screamed as the fireflies' light overwhelmed them, and Tharion's roar of fury echoed through the Citadel. The darkness that had once threatened to consume them was breaking, shattering under the weight of the fireflies' power.

And in that moment, Cassian knew—they were winning.

Chapter 35: The Last Light

The air around them crackled with energy, the fireflies' light surging with newfound strength as Cassian, Lyra, and Orion stood side by side. The darkness that had once suffocated the Citadel was breaking apart, but Tharion's presence still loomed, his fury palpable. His voice echoed through the chamber, filled with raw anger and disbelief.

"You think you can defy me?" Tharion roared, his form shifting like a living shadow. "I am the darkness that has existed long before the fireflies' pathetic light. You are nothing!"

Cassian's heart pounded in his chest as he felt the fireflies' magic coursing through him, stronger than before, but he knew they were nearing their limit. Tharion's power was ancient, relentless, and even as they pushed him back, the battle was far from over.

"We're not nothing," Lyra said, her voice trembling with emotion, yet filled with determination. "We're the light that will never fade."

With a sharp breath, Lyra raised her flute once more, her melody piercing through the air like a blade of light. The fireflies responded to her call, their glow intensifying as they swarmed around the siblings, creating a shield of golden light that held Tharion's darkness at bay.

Orion stepped forward, his sword gleaming in the fireflies' glow, his eyes fixed on the towering figure of Tharion. "You've lost, Tharion," he growled, his voice filled with defiance. "The fireflies are stronger than you."

Tharion's eyes blazed with fury, and the shadows around him surged, twisting, and writhing as they lashed out at the siblings. The darkness seemed to take on a life of its own, reaching for them like claws, determined to snuff out their light.

But Cassian, Lyra, and Orion stood firm, their hearts bound to the fireflies' magic. They could feel the warmth of the light pulsing through their veins, their connection to the fireflies deepening with every passing moment.

"Now, Cassian!" Lyra shouted, her voice filled with urgency. "Use the crystal!"

Cassian nodded, his grip tightening around the crystal that held the fireflies' magic. He could feel their energy thrumming within it, alive and powerful, but he knew this would be their final chance to defeat Tharion. The fireflies had given them everything they had, and now It was up to him to wield that power.

With a deep breath, Cassian raised the crystal high above his head, his voice steady as he called on the fireflies' magic one last time. "Fireflies of the heart," he whispered, repeating the words of the poem. "Guide us through the darkness."

The crystal flared to life, its light blazing brighter than ever before. The fireflies' magic surged through the chamber, filling every corner with golden brilliance. The shadows recoiled, hissing as they were consumed by the overwhelming light.

Tharion screamed in fury, his form distorting as the fireflies' light enveloped him. "No! This cannot be!"

But Cassian, Lyra, and Orion held strong, their hearts united with the fireflies. The light burned brighter, stronger, pushing back the darkness until there was nothing left but a blinding radiance. The fireflies' magic was like a living force, flowing through them, protecting them, and guiding them.

"You will never destroy the fireflies," Cassian shouted, his voice echoing through the chamber. "They live on through us!"

Tharion's form began to unravel, his dark energy collapsing under the weight of the fireflies' power. His voice, once so strong and menacing, grew weaker, filled with desperation. "You... cannot... win..."

But it was too late. The fireflies' light had already won.

With one final burst of energy, the shadows that clung to Tharion disintegrated, and his form shattered like glass, scattering into the air as the fireflies' light consumed him completely. The darkness that had plagued the Citadel for so long was gone, wiped away by the purity of the fireflies' magic.

The silence that followed was deafening.

Cassian stood frozen, the crystal still glowing faintly in his hand. The golden light of the fireflies filled the chamber, but the oppressive weight of Tharion's presence was gone. For the first time in what felt like an eternity, the Citadel was free of his dark influence.

"We... we did it," Lyra whispered, her voice filled with awe.

Orion lowered his sword, his chest heaving with exhaustion. "It's over."

Cassian's knees nearly gave out as the adrenaline left his body, the exhaustion of the battle crashing down on him. He could still feel the fireflies' magic pulsing through him, but it was gentler now, no longer the fierce, blinding force it had been moments before.

The fireflies fluttered around them, their soft glow illuminating the ruins of the Citadel. Their light was calm, peaceful, as if they were thanking the siblings for saving them.

Cassian's heart swelled with emotion as he looked at his siblings, Lyra's face pale with relief, and Orion's expression finally softening after the long, hard battle. They had survived. They had won.

"The fireflies..." Cassian whispered, his voice trembling. "They're still with us."

Lyra's eyes filled with tears as she nodded. "They always will be."

The fireflies swirled around them, their golden glow brightening the room. They had been through so much facing the darkness, confronting their fears, and sacrificing everything to protect the fireflies' magic. But now, standing in the heart of the Citadel, they knew they had done it. They had saved the fireflies, and in doing so, they had saved the light that their mother had fought so hard to protect.

As they stood there, bathed in the fireflies' light, Cassian could feel a deep sense of peace settling over him. The darkness had been vanquished, and the fireflies' magic had been restored.

But he also knew that their journey was not over. There were still many challenges ahead, and the Citadel needed rebuilding. The fireflies, though safe for now, would need their protection in the days to come.

"We have a lot of work to do," Cassian said softly, his voice filled with quiet resolve. "But we'll do it together."

Lyra and Orion nodded, their eyes filled with the same determination.

Together, they walked forward, leaving the vault behind as the fireflies' light guided them toward the future.

Chapter 36: The Aftermath

The golden glow of the fireflies illuminated the ruins of the Citadel as Cassian, Lyra, and Orion stood at the heart of what had once been a place of strength and magic. The battle with Tharion had left the ancient structure scarred cracks ran deep through the stone, and the air still carried the faint echo of the darkness that had plagued it. But for the first time in what felt like an eternity, the oppressive weight of Tharion's presence was gone.

Cassian ran a hand through his hair, his eyes scanning the damaged walls of the Citadel. The fireflies fluttered around them, their light soft and comforting, but there was an undeniable sense of fragility in the air. Though Tharion had been defeated, the Citadel was far from being whole again.

"We've won the battle, but the war isn't over," Cassian muttered under his breath, his gaze fixed on the shattered stone before him.

Lyra knelt beside him, her flute resting in her lap as she gently touched the cracked floor. "The fireflies' magic is back, but it is weak. The Citadel... it feels like it is barely holding together."

Orion stood nearby, his sword still in hand, though the immediate danger had passed. He glanced at his siblings, his expression grim. "We may have driven Tharion away but look around. The Citadel is falling apart. If we do not act fast, everything our mother fought for will be lost."

Cassian's heart tightened at the mention of their mother. Her legacy, the fireflies' magic, and everything she had protected was now in their hands. But the weight of that responsibility was overwhelming.

How were they supposed to restore the Citadel when so much had been destroyed?

"We'll need help," Cassian said after a long pause. "The three of us can't rebuild this place on our own."

Lyra nodded in agreement. "We will need to call the Luminaires. They can help us repair the damage, and maybe... maybe there is more about the fireflies that we do not know. The Citadel holds many secrets."

Orion sheathed his sword, his eyes narrowing thoughtfully. "The Luminaires will come, but even they will not be enough. We will need more than just strength. The fireflies' magic is tied to something deeper in the Citadel, something ancient."

Cassian's pulse quickened at Orion's words. He had felt it too—that the fireflies were more than just a source of light and magic. Their connection to the Citadel, to their mother, and to something even older had always been a mystery. Perhaps now was the time to uncover that mystery.

"We need to learn everything we can about the fireflies," Cassian said, determination filling his voice. "Whatever power they hold, we need to understand it. There is more at stake here than just the Citadel. Tharion's darkness might be gone, but there could be more threats we do not see yet."

Lyra's face paled slightly at the thought. "You think there is more out there? More like Tharion?"

Cassian sighed, his gaze drifting toward the flickering fireflies. "I do not know. But I do not want to take any chances."

Before any of them could respond, a low rumble echoed through the Citadel, sending a tremor through the ground. The siblings exchanged nervous glances as the walls of the ancient structure groaned under the strain of the recent battle.

"We don't have much time," Orion said, his voice sharp. "The Citadel is unstable. If we do not reinforce it soon, it could collapse."

Lyra stood quickly, her face filled with determination. "Then we should start now. I will reach out to the Luminaires and gather as many as I can. They will know how to stabilize the Citadel."

"I'll scout the surrounding areas," Orion added. "Make sure there are not any lingering traces of Tharion's magic. We cannot afford to be caught off guard."

Cassian nodded, appreciating their readiness to act, but there was a gnawing feeling in his chest that something else was waiting for them—something hidden in the ruins of the Citadel. The fireflies' magic was ancient, far older than he or his siblings knew, and he had a sense that they had only scratched the surface of its true power.

As Lyra and Orion prepared to leave, Cassian lingered in the center of the chamber, his eyes drawn to the fireflies that floated above him, their glow soft and delicate.

There is something more here, he thought, his mind racing. Something we have not yet discovered.

The fireflies' light pulsed faintly, as if responding to his thoughts, and for a brief moment, Cassian felt a connection—a whisper, like a voice from long ago, telling him to look deeper.

Suddenly, a soft voice broke the silence, causing Cassian to turn.

"You're right, you know," said a figure emerging from the shadows.

Cassian's heart leapt as he recognized the man—Master Eryndor, one of the elder Luminaires and a former mentor to the siblings. His presence was both reassuring and unexpected, as Eryndor had been missing during the battle with Tharion.

"You felt it, didn't you?" Eryndor continued, his voice calm but serious. "The fireflies' magic is only a piece of the puzzle. There is something much older tied to this place, something that even your mother did not fully understand."

Cassian narrowed his eyes, his pulse quickening. "What are you talking about?"

Eryndor stepped closer, his expression unreadable. "There is a force within the Citadel, hidden deep beneath its foundations. A power older than the fireflies, older than the Citadel itself. It has been dormant for centuries, but Tharion's attack may have stirred it."

Lyra and Orion exchanged wary glances as they approached. "Why didn't you tell us this before?" Orion asked, his voice laced with suspicion.

Eryndor smiled faintly. "Because even I did not fully understand it until now. Tharion's attack may have weakened the fireflies, but it also revealed something that was hidden—a power that could either restore the Citadel or destroy it."

Cassian's breath caught in his throat. "And you think this power is still here?"

Eryndor nodded. "Yes. And if we are to truly save the Citadel, we must find it before it is too late."

Chapter 37: Beneath the Surface

The weight of Eryndor's words hung heavily in the air. Cassian felt the fireflies' soft glow around him, but the peacefulness of their light now seemed fragile, almost temporary. There was something more—something older and darker beneath the surface of the Citadel.

Lyra's face had paled since Eryndor's revelation. "An ancient power?" she asked quietly, her voice trembling. "What could be more powerful than the fireflies? What could be older than the Citadel?"

Eryndor's expression was unreadable as he stepped closer. "It is a force that has been dormant for centuries. Your mother and I suspected its presence long ago, but it was never confirmed. We believed the fireflies were the key to protecting the Citadel, but now I realize that the fireflies are merely a part of a much larger puzzle."

Orion's eyes narrowed as he studied the elder Luminaire. "And this power, you're saying it could destroy the Citadel if we disturb it?"

Eryndor nodded solemnly. "It is possible. But it is also possible that this power could be the key to fully restoring the fireflies' strength—and even more. Tharion's attack weakened the fireflies, but it also revealed the cracks in the Citadel's foundation, both literal and magical."

Cassian's pulse quickened as he processed the implications. If there was truly an ancient force beneath the Citadel, it could explain the fragile state of the fireflies' magic. But was it worth the risk to pursue something they barely understood?

"We don't have time to debate this," Orion said, his voice tense. "The Citadel is already unstable. If we start poking around for some hidden power, we could make things worse."

Lyra shifted uneasily beside him. "But if this power can restore the fireflies, we cannot ignore it. We need to understand what we are dealing with."

Cassian clenched his fists, feeling the weight of the decision pressing down on him. The Citadel was their responsibility now, and the fireflies were depending on them. But Eryndor's words raised more questions than answers. Could they risk searching for a power that might be more dangerous than Tharion?

"What do you think, Eryndor?" Cassian asked, his voice filled with uncertainty. "If we try to uncover this power, could it really help us restore the Citadel?"

Eryndor's gaze softened, his voice calm. "I believe it could. But it will not be easy. The path to the source of this power is hidden deep beneath the Citadel, in places that have not been touched in generations. It is a dangerous journey, but it may be the only way to fully protect the fireflies."

Lyra bit her lip, her eyes filled with worry. "And if we leave it alone? What happens then?"

Eryndor hesitated. "The power will remain dormant—for now. But with the Citadel already weakened, there is no guarantee it will stay that way. If it awakens on its own, we will not be prepared."

Cassian exchanged a glance with Lyra and Orion. This was their decision to make, but every option seemed filled with risk.

"We have to try," Cassian finally said, his voice steady with resolve. "We can't leave something this powerful hidden beneath the Citadel, especially if it could help us save the fireflies."

Orion's jaw tightened, but he nodded in agreement. "If we are going to do this, we need a plan. We do not even know where to start looking."

Eryndor stepped forward, his voice low. "I can help with that. There are old maps of the Citadel—ones that show the hidden passages that lead to the lower levels. Your mother and I discovered those years ago, but we never had the chance to explore them fully."

Cassian's heart pounded. The idea of venturing into the unknown depths of the Citadel, where an ancient and potentially dangerous power lay dormant, was terrifying. But he also knew it was necessary. They could not rebuild the Citadel properly without understanding what was beneath it.

"Show us the way," Cassian said, his voice filled with determination.

Eryndor nodded, turning toward one of the side chambers. "The maps are stored in the Hall of Archives. Follow me."

As they moved through the Citadel, the damage from Tharion's attack was painfully clear. The once grand halls were cracked and crumbling, and the fireflies' light, though restored, was dimmer than it should have been. Cassian felt a knot of anxiety growing in his chest. They had saved the fireflies, but they had not truly won—not yet.

When they reached the Hall of Archives, Cassian felt a sense of reverence wash over him. The vast chamber was filled with ancient tomes and scrolls, remnants of the Citadel's long history. Eryndor moved with purpose, searching through the shelves until he found what he was looking for—a large, rolled-up map, its edges worn with age.

"This map shows the oldest parts of the Citadel," Eryndor explained as he unrolled it on the table. "These lower levels have not been touched in centuries. It is likely that the source of the power lies deep within these tunnels."

Cassian studied the map, his eyes tracing the winding passageways that led far beneath the Citadel. The thought of venturing so deep into the unknown sent a chill down his spine, but he knew they had no choice.

"We'll need to be prepared," Orion said, his voice firm. "These tunnels could be dangerous. Who knows what is down there after all these years?"

Lyra nodded, her expression serious. "And we will need to protect the fireflies while we are down there. If their magic falters again..."

"We won't let that happen," Cassian interrupted, his voice filled with conviction. "We've come too far to let the fireflies' light fade now."

Eryndor looked at them, his gaze filled with a quiet respect. "You have grown stronger than I imagined. Your mother would be proud."

Cassian swallowed hard, the mention of their mother bringing a flood of emotions to the surface. She had sacrificed everything to protect the fireflies, and now it was their turn to do the same.

"We'll make sure her legacy lives on," Cassian said softly.

With the map in hand, the siblings began preparing for the journey ahead. They gathered supplies, weapons, and anything they might need for the dangerous descent into the unknown depths of the Citadel.

As they stood at the entrance to the lower levels, the air felt heavy with anticipation. The fireflies hovered around them, their light flickering softly as if sensing the uncertainty of what lay ahead.

"This is it," Cassian said, his voice steady but filled with tension. "Whatever is down there, we'll face it together."

Lyra nodded, her hand gripping her flute tightly. "We're ready."

Orion drew his sword, his eyes fixed on the dark passage before them. "Let's go."

With a deep breath, Cassian led the way, the map clutched tightly in his hand as they descended into the depths of the Citadel, where ancient secrets and untold dangers awaited.

Chapter 38: The Guardian of the Depths

The deeper the siblings descended into the Citadel, the more the air around them thickened with an ancient, unspoken presence. The fireflies' light flickered softly, guiding them through the dark, twisting passageways that had been untouched for centuries. The map in Cassian's hand showed the labyrinth of tunnels below the Citadel, but even with Eryndor's guidance, the siblings felt the weight of the unknown pressing down on them.

Lyra shivered as they passed through another narrow corridor, her flute clutched tightly in her hand. "It feels like the walls are watching us," she whispered, her voice barely audible over the echo of their footsteps.

Orion's grip on his sword tightened as he glanced around warily. "Whatever this ancient power is, we need to be careful. There is no telling what we will find down here."

Cassian nodded, his eyes fixed on the glowing path ahead. The fireflies had been their constant companions through this journey, but now their light felt different—brighter, more intense. It was as if they were leading the siblings toward something, or someone.

"There's something ahead," Eryndor said quietly, his voice filled with a strange reverence. "The fireflies are guiding us to the heart of the Citadel."

As they moved deeper into the passageway, the walls seemed to hum with energy, and the faint glow of the fireflies illuminated a vast chamber up ahead. The siblings exchanged tense glances as they stepped into the open space, their breath catching in their throats.

The chamber was enormous, its ceiling arching high above them, covered in ancient runes and carvings. In the center of the room stood a massive stone structure, shaped like a hollowed-out tree, its surface glowing with the same golden light as the fireflies. But what caught their attention was the figure standing before it—an ethereal being with wings that shimmered like the fireflies' glow.

Cassian's heart raced as he recognized the figure. "Eldrin..."

Lyra gasped, her eyes wide with awe. "He's here."

The ancient firefly guardian, Eldrin, stood before them, his form both solid and spectral, as if he existed between worlds. His wings, once bright and vibrant, now flickered faintly, as though they were running out of time. His eyes, filled with centuries of wisdom and sorrow, met Cassian's, and a deep understanding passed between them.

"You've come," Eldrin said softly, his voice carrying the weight of ages. "Just as your mother once did."

Cassian stepped forward, his heart pounding in his chest. "Eldrin... we have been looking for you. We need your help. The fireflies' magic—"

"I know," Eldrin interrupted gently. "The fireflies' light has been fading, and you have restored much of it. But there is more at stake here than you realize."

Eryndor, standing beside the siblings, bowed his head in respect. "Eldrin, you have guarded the ancient power beneath the Citadel for centuries. We need to understand its nature, and whether it can be controlled."

Eldrin's wings fluttered weakly, and he looked toward the massive stone tree in the center of the chamber. "This power is not something to be controlled," he said quietly. "It is a force older than the Citadel itself, tied to the very essence of the fireflies' magic. I have spent centuries guarding it, keeping it contained. But now, it has begun to awaken."

Lyra's voice trembled as she spoke. "Why is it awakening now? Did Tharion cause this?"

Eldrin's gaze darkened. "Tharion's corruption weakened the barriers that kept this power dormant. But even before his attack, the balance of magic had begun to shift. The fireflies are connected to this power, and as their light dimmed, the ancient force stirred."

Orion stepped forward, his brow furrowed. "And if it fully awakens? What happens then?"

Eldrin closed his eyes for a moment, his wings drooping. "If it awakens without guidance, it could consume everything—the fireflies, the Citadel, even the world beyond. This force is not inherently evil, but it is vast and untamed. It needs to be anchored, controlled by those who understand its nature."

Cassian felt a knot of fear tighten in his chest. "And you're the one who's been keeping it in check?"

Eldrin nodded slowly. "For centuries, I have been bound to this power, keeping it contained. But I am weakening. The fireflies' light, while restored, is not enough to hold it back any longer."

Lyra's eyes filled with concern. "Then what do we do? How can we stop it?"

Eldrin looked at the siblings, his expression softening. "You are the key. Your connection to the fireflies, to the legacy of your mother—it is stronger than you realize. If you can harness the fireflies' magic, you may be able to anchor this power, to give it form and purpose. But it will not be easy."

Cassian swallowed hard, the weight of responsibility pressing down on him. "What do we need to do?"

Eldrin gestured to the glowing tree-like structure in the center of the chamber. "This is the heart of the ancient power. You must use the fireflies' magic to connect with it, to bind it to you. If you succeed, the fireflies will grow stronger, and the Citadel will be restored. But if you fail... the power will be unleashed, and there will be no stopping it."

Orion glanced at Cassian, his expression grim. "This is a huge risk. If we do not do this right..."

Cassian nodded, his heart pounding. "I know. But we have to try."

Lyra took a deep breath, her eyes filled with determination. "We have come this far. We cannot turn back now."

Eldrin smiled faintly, though his wings continued to flicker with weakness. "Your mother believed in you, and so do I. You are the last hope of the fireflies."

With those words, Cassian stepped forward, feeling the fireflies' magic thrumming in his veins. Lyra and Orion followed, their resolve unwavering. Together, they stood before the heart of the ancient power, the fireflies swirling around them, their light brighter than ever before.

As they prepared to connect with the ancient force, Cassian felt a deep sense of purpose settling over him. This was what they were meant to do—for what their mother had prepared them. The fate of the fireflies, the Citadel, and perhaps the world itself, rested in their hands.

And there was no turning back.

Chapter 39: The Heart of the Power

Cassian's heart pounded in his chest as he stood before the glowing, tree-like structure that radiated with ancient energy. The air around them felt charged with a force older than anything he had ever known—vast, untamed, and dangerous. The fireflies fluttered in the air, their light bright but delicate, as if sensing the magnitude of the task ahead.

Eldrin's weak voice echoed through the chamber, his wings fluttering faintly. "You must approach the heart with caution. The power that lies within is not something to be taken lightly. It will test you. Only those with a deep connection to the fireflies can withstand its pull."

Cassian exchanged a glance with Lyra and Orion, his pulse quickening. They had faced so much already—Tharion, the threat of the Citadel's collapse—but this felt different. The weight of the ancient power pressed down on them like a heavy fog, and for the first time, Cassian wondered if they were truly ready for this.

"What do we need to do?" Lyra asked softly, her voice trembling with a mixture of fear and resolve.

Eldrin closed his eyes, his expression one of deep focus. "You must use the fireflies' magic to connect with the heart of this power. Each of you carries a piece of that magic within you—passed down through your mother's legacy. The fireflies will guide you, but you must be willing to open yourself fully to their light."

Orion gripped the hilt of his sword tightly, his eyes dark with concern. "And if we fail?"

Eldrin's wings drooped further, his voice barely more than a whisper. "If you fail, the power will be unleashed in its raw, uncontrollable form. It will consume the fireflies' magic, the Citadel, and everything connected to it. You must succeed."

Cassian felt a knot of fear tighten in his chest. The responsibility of what lay before them was overwhelming. If they made even one wrong move, they could lose everything—the Citadel, the fireflies, and the legacy their mother had fought so hard to protect.

"We've faced worse," Orion muttered, trying to sound confident. "We can handle this."

But Cassian could hear the uncertainty in his brother's voice. This was different from any battle they had fought before. This was a battle of the soul—of magic and trust.

Lyra stepped forward, her flute raised as she took a deep breath. "I'll go first."

Cassian's heart leapt into his throat. "Lyra, wait—"

But Lyra shook her head, her eyes filled with a quiet determination. "The fireflies have always been drawn to music. I can feel them responding to my flute. If we are going to connect with this power, we need to trust in the magic they have given us."

With that, Lyra began to play a soft, haunting melody, the notes echoing through the chamber like whispers in the dark. The fireflies responded instantly, their light pulsing in time with the music, growing brighter and more vibrant. Cassian and Orion watched in awe as the fireflies swirled around Lyra, their golden glow enveloping her in a cocoon of light.

As the melody filled the air, Lyra stepped closer to the heart of the ancient power, her movements slow and deliberate. The tree-like structure pulsed with energy, its roots glowing as they seemed to come to life, reaching toward her like tendrils of light. The fireflies guided her steps, their magic intertwining with the ancient force that lay dormant within the heart.

Cassian held his breath, his eyes locked on Lyra as she approached the center of the structure. The air around them crackled with energy, and he could feel the ancient power pulling at the edges of his mind, tempting him to give in.

But Lyra remained calm, her melody steady and unwavering.

As she reached the heart, the light surrounding her flared, and for a moment, the entire chamber was bathed in brilliant golden light. Cassian shielded his eyes, the intensity of the fireflies' magic nearly overwhelming.

When the light faded, Lyra stood at the center of the glowing tree, her eyes closed, her flute still raised. The fireflies swirled around her in a dazzling display of light, and Cassian could feel the connection she had made with the ancient power.

But something was wrong.

The roots of the tree began to pulse more violently, their glow turning darker, more unstable. Lyra's melody faltered, and her face twisted in pain as the fireflies' light flickered around her.

"Lyra!" Cassian shouted, rushing toward her. "What's happening?"

Eldrin's voice was weak but urgent. "The power is resisting! She is too close to the heart—it is too much for her to control on her own!"

Orion cursed under his breath, his sword raised as he looked toward the tree. "We need to help her!"

Without hesitation, Cassian and Orion stepped forward, their hearts pounding as they felt the ancient power pulling at them, tugging at their very souls. The fireflies' light flickered around them, but it was weaker now, as if the power of the heart were overwhelming their magic.

Cassian's pulse quickened as he reached Lyra's side, his hand gripping the crystal that held the fireflies' magic. "We'll do this together," he whispered, his voice filled with determination.

Orion stepped to Lyra's other side, his sword glowing faintly with the fireflies' light. "Let's finish this."

Together, the siblings reached out, their hands touching the glowing roots of the tree. The moment their hands made contact, a surge of energy rushed through them, filling their bodies with the raw, untamed power of the ancient force. The fireflies' magic flared to life, pushing back against the dark energy that threatened to consume them.

Cassian felt the pull of the ancient power deep within him, a force that seemed to stretch beyond time and space. It was vast, infinite, and dangerous, but there was also something beautiful about it—a potential for creation, for growth, if they could only harness it.

"We have to trust the fireflies," Cassian said through gritted teeth, his mind racing as he tried to keep control. "They're the key."

Lyra's voice trembled as she continued to play, the fireflies responding to her melody with renewed strength. "We can do this. We just need to stay connected—to the fireflies, to each other."

Orion's grip on his sword tightened, his face set with determination. "We will not let this thing control us. We are stronger than it."

As the siblings focused on the fireflies' light, the ancient power began to shift, its wild energy slowly bending to their will. The tree's roots glowed brighter, and the dark energy that had threatened to overwhelm them began to recede.

Cassian felt a surge of hope. They were doing it. They were controlling the power.

But just as the ancient force began to stabilize, a low, rumbling voice echoed through the chamber, filled with malice and fury.

"You cannot control what you do not understand."

Cassian's blood ran cold as the shadows in the chamber began to twist and writhe, coiling together to form a familiar, menacing figure—Tharion.

His eyes burned with dark fire as he stepped toward the glowing tree, his presence sending a wave of darkness through the chamber.

"You thought you could defeat me," Tharion sneered, his voice dripping with contempt. "But this power was never yours to control."

Cassian's heart raced as he realized the truth. Tharion had not been defeated—he had been waiting, lurking in the shadows, waiting for them to make this very mistake.

"Tharion!" Orion growled, raising his sword. "You're not taking this power!"

But Tharion's smile only widened. "You are children playing with forces far beyond your understanding. And now, you will suffer the consequences."

The chamber trembled as Tharion's dark magic surged toward them, threatening to undo everything for which they had fought.

Cassian's pulse quickened as he felt the ancient power slipping out of their control. They were running out of time.

"Stay focused!" Cassian shouted, his voice filled with desperation. "We can still do this!"

But even as he said the words, he knew the last battle had only just begun.

Chapter 40: The Return of Darkness

The air in the chamber seemed to freeze as Tharion's dark presence flooded the space. His figure, tall and menacing, loomed over the siblings, his eyes glowing with an eerie, malevolent light. The fireflies' glow flickered uncertainly, their golden light fighting against the shadows that swirled around them.

Cassian's breath caught in his throat as he felt the ancient power slipping from their grasp. The wild energy they had been trying to control was now thrumming with instability, and Tharion's dark magic only made it more dangerous.

"You can't control this power," Tharion sneered, his voice filled with contempt. "It was never meant for you."

Orion's jaw tightened, his sword raised as he stepped in front of Lyra and Cassian. "We won't let you take it."

Tharion's laughter echoed through the chamber, cold and mocking. "You are fools, all of you. Do you really think you can stop me? This power is beyond your understanding. It belongs to me."

Cassian's heart pounded in his chest. Tharion had been waiting in the shadows, lurking, and now that they had tried to harness the ancient force, he had returned to claim it. The fireflies' magic was their only defense, but even that felt fragile against the overwhelming darkness.

"Cassian," Lyra whispered, her voice trembling with fear. "What do we do?"

Cassian's mind raced as he gripped the crystal that held the fireflies' magic. He could feel the ancient power surging through the glowing tree-like structure, wild and untamed. If they did not act fast, Tharion would seize control of it, and everything they had fought for would be lost.

"We have to keep the fireflies' magic strong," Cassian said, his voice filled with urgency. "It's the only thing that can stop him."

Lyra nodded, raising her flute once more, though her hands shook with fear. She began to play a slow, haunting melody, the notes filling the chamber with a fragile sense of hope. The fireflies responded immediately, their light flaring brighter, pushing back the shadows that swirled around them.

But Tharion was relentless.

With a wave of his hand, the shadows surged forward, lashing out toward the siblings with violent force. Orion stepped in front of Lyra, his sword cutting through the darkness, but each strike felt heavier than the last, as if the shadows were feeding off his strength.

"You cannot defeat me," Tharion snarled, his voice echoing through the chamber. "This power is mine. You are nothing but children playing with forces you cannot comprehend."

Cassian's grip tightened on the crystal, his pulse racing. He could feel the fireflies' magic responding to Lyra's melody, but it was not enough. The ancient power was still too wild, too dangerous, and Tharion's influence was making it even harder to control.

"We have to do this together," Cassian said, his voice filled with determination. "The fireflies' magic—if we combine it, we can stop him."

Orion glanced at him, his face lined with tension. "How? He is too strong!"

Cassian's mind raced. The fireflies' light was the only thing keeping Tharion at bay, but they needed to find a way to focus it, to channel it into the ancient power and take control before Tharion could.

"Lyra," Cassian said, his voice steady. "Play the melody our mother taught us—the one that connects the fireflies to the heart of the Citadel. It is the only way."

Lyra's eyes widened, but she nodded, her face pale with fear. "I'll try."

With trembling hands, Lyra shifted the notes of her melody, the sound shifting from haunting to something deeper, more resonant. The fireflies responded immediately, their light growing brighter and more focused. Cassian could feel the magic in the air, the fireflies' energy binding together in a way he had not felt before.

Tharion's eyes narrowed as he sensed the change. "What are you doing?"

"We're ending this," Cassian said, his voice firm.

As Lyra played, the fireflies' light began to gather around the glowing tree at the center of the chamber. The wild, untamed energy of the ancient power started to calm, its pulsing light growing steadier, more controlled. The fireflies' magic was intertwining with it, binding it to their will.

Cassian stepped forward, holding the crystal high as the fireflies' light surged through him. The crystal blazed with golden light, and for a moment, he felt a deep connection to the ancient power, as if it were part of him.

"We have to trust the fireflies," Cassian whispered, his voice filled with conviction. "They've guided us this far—they won't let us fail."

Orion stood beside him, his sword glowing with the fireflies' light. "We're with you."

Together, the siblings reached out, their hands touching the glowing tree. The moment their hands made contact, a surge of energy rushed through them, filling them with the full force of the ancient power. The fireflies' magic flared brighter than ever before, binding the ancient force to them, controlling it.

Tharion's scream of rage filled the chamber as he realized what was happening. "No! You cannot take this from me!"

But it was too late. The fireflies' light surged through the ancient power, pushing back Tharion's darkness with overwhelming force. The shadows that had surrounded them began to disintegrate, dissolving into nothing as the fireflies' magic overwhelmed them.

Cassian could feel the fireflies' energy coursing through him, filling every corner of the chamber with brilliant golden light. The ancient power, once wild and dangerous, was now under their control, its energy flowing in harmony with the fireflies' magic.

Tharion staggered back, his form flickering as the fireflies' light consumed him. His eyes burned with fury, but there was nothing he could do. The siblings had taken control of the ancient power, and his darkness was no match for their combined strength.

"This isn't over," Tharion snarled, his voice weak but filled with malice. "I will return. I will always return."

Cassian's grip on the crystal tightened, his heart pounding. "Not this time."

With one final surge of energy, the fireflies' light exploded outward, filling the chamber with blinding brilliance. Tharion's form shattered, his dark magic disintegrating under the weight of the fireflies' power.

And then, there was silence.

The chamber was bathed in golden light, the fireflies fluttering softly around them. The ancient power, once wild and untamed, now pulsed with a steady, controlled energy. The Citadel was safe—for now.

Cassian's knees buckled as the adrenaline left his body, and he collapsed to the ground, gasping for breath. Lyra and Orion rushed to his side, their faces pale with exhaustion, but their eyes filled with relief.

"We did it," Lyra whispered, her voice trembling with emotion. "We really did it."

Orion nodded, his chest heaving. "Tharion's gone. For good this time."

Cassian closed his eyes, letting the warmth of the fireflies' light wash over him. They had won. The Citadel was safe, the fireflies' magic restored, and the ancient power now under their control.

But even as he felt the weight of victory settle over him, Cassian knew their journey was not over. The fireflies would need their protection, and there were still many mysteries about the Citadel that had yet to be uncovered.

"We'll rebuild," Cassian said softly, his voice filled with quiet determination. "We'll make sure the fireflies' light never fades again."

Lyra smiled weakly, her eyes filled with hope. "We will do it. Together."

As the siblings stood in the heart of the Citadel, surrounded by the fireflies' light, they knew that no matter what challenges lay ahead, they would face them together. The fireflies had guided them this far, and they would continue to light their path.

And as long as the fireflies' light burned, the Citadel would endure.

Chapter 41: A Fragile Peace

The Citadel stood in quiet stillness, its walls bathed in the soft, flickering glow of the fireflies. Their golden light, once nearly extinguished, now hovered like delicate embers in the air, filling the vast chamber with a sense of fragile peace. Yet beneath that tranquility, Cassian, Lyra, and Orion could feel it—the tension, the weight of something much larger than themselves.

Cassian stood at the center of the chamber, his hands still trembling from the strain of the battle they had just survived. The fireflies had been saved, and the ancient power, once wild and dangerous, had been bound to them. But that victory felt fleeting, as if it could unravel at any moment.

"We did it," Lyra whispered, her voice soft as she stared at the swirling fireflies. "The fireflies are safe... for now."

Orion, standing beside her, was less convinced. His arms crossed over his chest, his eyes never leaving the cracks in the stone walls around them. "But for how long?" His voice was low, edged with worry. "We have tapped into something we barely understand. What is stopping it from turning against us?"

Eryndor, who had remained silent since the battle's end, stepped forward. His once-confident presence was now tempered by the weight of the ancient power they had unleashed. "The power you have awakened is not evil, but it is untamed. It has been dormant for centuries, and in binding it to the fireflies, you have altered the very magic that sustains this place."

Cassian turned to him, his chest tightening at Eryndor's words. "Are we in danger?"

Eryndor met his gaze, his expression grave. "Not immediately. But the balance is delicate. The fireflies are now tied to something much greater than their original magic. It will take time to fully understand what you have awakened, and until then, you must tread carefully."

Lyra took a step closer, her voice filled with concern. "What if we lose control? What if we cannot contain it?"

Eryndor hesitated, his eyes flicking toward the fireflies that hovered above them. "If you lose control... the consequences could be catastrophic. The ancient power could overwhelm the fireflies, consuming their magic and everything connected to it—the Citadel, the land beyond."

Orion's expression darkened. "So, we have not really won. We have just delayed the inevitable."

"No," Cassian said, his voice firmer than he felt. "We have given ourselves a chance. That is what this is. A chance to rebuild, to strengthen the Citadel, and to learn how to control the power we have unlocked."

Eryndor nodded slowly, though the worry in his eyes remained. "You are right. This is a chance, but it is also a responsibility. The Citadel has always been a sanctuary for the fireflies, but now it is something more. It is a beacon of immense power. And others will notice."

Lyra glanced at Cassian, her brow furrowed. "What do you mean? Are we... in danger from outside the Citadel?"

Eryndor's voice was heavy with warning. "Yes. Now that the fireflies are bound to this ancient force, it will draw attention. Those who seek power will come. The magic you have awakened will be like a beacon to them, and they will stop at nothing to claim it."

Orion's jaw clenched, his hand resting on the hilt of his sword. "Then we will fight. We will protect the Citadel."

Cassian felt a cold knot of fear settle in his stomach. They had fought so hard to save the fireflies from Tharion, only to find themselves facing new threats, ones they had not even anticipated. The ancient power, though controlled for now, was a double-edged sword, and he was not sure they fully understood what they had unlocked.

"We need to be smart about this," Cassian said, his voice quieter now. "We cannot just focus on rebuilding the walls. We need to strengthen our understanding of the magic we have bound ourselves to. If we do not, we will be vulnerable."

Lyra nodded, her face pale but determined. "We can call on the Luminaires. They have studied the fireflies' magic for centuries. They can help us understand this new connection."

Eryndor's expression softened slightly at Lyra's words. "The Luminaires will come. But they do not fully comprehend the ancient power that now flows through the Citadel. This is uncharted territory. You will need to be cautious."

Orion's eyes narrowed as he studied the crumbling walls of the Citadel. "And what if they come? The ones who seek power. How do we defend against that?"

Eryndor was silent for a moment before answering. "You must fortify the Citadel, not just with stone and magic, but with understanding. The fireflies' light is your greatest weapon, but only if you can wield it. Those who come for the power you have uncovered will be relentless."

Cassian took a deep breath, his heart pounding with the weight of Eryndor's words. The Citadel was no longer just a sanctuary—it was a battleground waiting to be claimed. And they were its only protectors.

"We'll defend it," Cassian said quietly, though the determination in his voice was clear. "Whatever it takes."

Orion nodded, his expression hardening. "We have faced worse. We will fight for this place."

Lyra smiled weakly, though her eyes were filled with uncertainty. "We have always fought together. That will not change."

Eryndor placed a hand on Cassian's shoulder, his gaze heavy with meaning. "Your mother believed in you, in your connection to the fireflies. She trusted that you would protect this place. But now, you are no longer just protectors. You are guardians of something far greater than any of us could have imagined."

Cassian swallowed hard, the enormity of the situation sinking in. They were no longer just saving the Citadel—they were safeguarding a power that could change everything. And with that power came enemies, ones who would stop at nothing to take it.

As the siblings stood in the heart of the Citadel, the fireflies fluttering softly around them, Cassian felt the weight of their future pressing down on him. They had won the battle, but the war was far from over. The ancient power they had awakened was vast, dangerous, and tied to them now. And soon, others would come for it.

"We'll rebuild," Cassian said softly, though his voice was filled with quiet resolve. "We will strengthen the Citadel, and we will protect the fireflies. No matter what comes next."

Lyra nodded, her gaze distant as she watched the fireflies dance through the air. "We'll be ready."

Orion tightened his grip on his sword, his expression determined. "Whatever it takes."

Eryndor gave them a final nod of approval. "The road ahead will not be easy. But you are the guardians now. The fireflies, the Citadel, this ancient power—they are in your hands."

As the fireflies' light flickered around them, Cassian, Lyra, and Orion stood together, their bond stronger than ever. They had saved the fireflies from Tharion, but in doing so, they had unlocked something far greater than they had anticipated.

And though the night was calm, in the depths of the Citadel, something stirred.

The ancient power they had awakened pulsed softly, waiting.

And soon, it would demand more than they were prepared to give.

Chapter 42: Rebuilding the Walls

The morning light filtered through the cracks in the Citadel's ancient stone walls, casting long shadows across the hallways where the battle with Tharion had once raged. Now, the Citadel was eerily quiet, save for the occasional flutter of fireflies weaving through the air. Their golden glow flickered softly, a reminder of the power that had saved them all—but also the force that had yet to reveal its full nature.

Cassian stood at the entrance to the main chamber, his eyes scanning the damage that Tharion's darkness had left behind. Broken pillars, crumbling stone, and scorch marks where shadows had lashed out during the battle. It was a stark reminder of the fragility of the fireflies' magic and the Citadel itself.

"We'll have to start with the walls," Orion said from behind him, his voice steady but weary. "If we don't reinforce the structure, the Citadel won't survive another attack—whether it's from inside or out."

Cassian nodded, his hands resting on the crystal that still hummed faintly with the fireflies' magic. "The fireflies' light is holding everything together for now, but you are right. We need to strengthen the Citadel, and fast."

Lyra appeared beside them, her brow furrowed as she studied the damaged hall. "The Luminaires are on their way. They will help with the rebuilding, but we need to prepare for more than just repairs. We need defenses—protection from whatever might come looking for this power."

Eryndor, standing quietly nearby, stepped forward. His eyes, though lined with exhaustion, still held a calm wisdom. "The Citadel has always been a sanctuary, but now it is something more. It is a beacon, and that means it will attract those who seek to control what you have unlocked. We must fortify both the structure and the magic."

Cassian's chest tightened at the thought. The Citadel had always felt like a place of safety, but now it was more vulnerable than ever. The fireflies' magic had been altered, bound to a force none of them fully understood. If anyone tried to take it from them, they could lose everything.

"The ancient power," Lyra said softly, her gaze distant. "Do you think we've truly contained it?"

Eryndor's expression darkened. "For now, it is bound to the fireflies' light, but its nature is unpredictable. You must stay vigilant, for even the smallest disturbance could awaken it once more."

Orion's eyes narrowed as he studied the crumbling stone. "Then we need to prepare for the worst."

Cassian turned to his brother, his heart heavy with the weight of the decision they faced. "We have no choice. The Citadel is all we have. If we do not protect it, everything our mother fought for will be lost."

Lyra sighed, her eyes filled with uncertainty. "It is more than just the Citadel now, though. The power we have tapped into—it feels... alive. Like it is waiting."

Eryndor's voice was low as he answered. "It is. The ancient power you have bound yourselves to is a living force, one that has existed for centuries. It is both a source of creation and destruction, and now that it is connected to the fireflies, it will demand more from you."

Cassian's pulse quickened at the thought. The battle with Tharion had been just the beginning. The real challenge would be learning to control what they had awakened before it consumed them.

"The Luminaires will help us understand it," Cassian said, his voice steadier than he felt. "And we'll rebuild the Citadel, stronger than it was before."

Orion nodded. "But we cannot just wait for them to arrive. We need to start now."

Cassian agreed. "Let us focus on reinforcing the outer walls. We will use the fireflies' magic to stabilize the structure, and when the Luminaires arrive, we will work on the deeper defenses."

As they began to plan the rebuilding, Cassian felt a growing sense of urgency. The Citadel's wounds were deep, and while the fireflies' magic had been restored, it was clear that their connection to the ancient power was fragile. Every decision they made from this point on would shape the future of the Citadel—and possibly the world beyond.

Hours passed as they worked to clear debris, gathering what materials they could to start rebuilding the outer walls. The fireflies fluttered around them, their light a constant but fragile presence, guiding them as they worked. Cassian could feel the fireflies' magic pulsing in time with the ancient power, a reminder that they were no longer simply protecting the fireflies—they were guarding something far more dangerous.

As they reinforced the main gates, Lyra paused, her gaze shifting to the horizon. "Do you think the Luminaires will know what we have done? That we've... changed the fireflies' magic?"

Eryndor, who had been overseeing their progress, answered with a sigh. "They will sense it. The fireflies' connection to this ancient force cannot be hidden. But whether they will understand it is another matter."

Cassian's heart sank at the thought. The Luminaires had always been the protectors of the fireflies' magic, but now, the siblings had bound that magic to a power that no one had foreseen. What would the Luminaires think? Would they view the siblings as saviors—or as a danger to everything they had built?

"We need their help," Cassian said, his voice low. "But we cannot let them take control. The fireflies are tied to us now. We are the ones who have to protect this place."

Orion nodded in agreement. "We'll work with the Luminaires, but we make the decisions."

Eryndor gave them a small nod of approval. "Your mother would be proud of your strength. You have taken on a burden that no one expected, and you have done so with wisdom. But remember, this power is still wild. It will test you, and it will demand more from you than you realize."

Cassian's chest tightened. He could feel the weight of that truth—an unsettling presence that lingered just beneath the surface. The ancient power was not done with them. It was waiting, watching, and testing the boundaries they had set.

"We'll be ready," Cassian said, though the uncertainty in his voice was clear.

As the sun began to set, casting long shadows over the Citadel, the siblings stood together at the edge of the crumbling walls. The fireflies' light flickered softly around them, but there was a new tension in the air, a sense that the quiet they had found was only temporary.

"We have a long road ahead," Lyra said softly, her eyes filled with both hope and fear. "But we're not alone."

Orion, ever the protector, placed a hand on his sword, his gaze steady. "We will protect this place. No matter what."

Cassian took a deep breath, his heart heavy with the responsibility they now carried. The Citadel was more than just a sanctuary for the fireflies—it was a beacon of immense power, one that others would seek to control. But as long as the siblings stood together, they would fight to protect it.

"We'll rebuild," Cassian said quietly, his voice filled with quiet determination. "And we'll be ready for whatever comes next."

The fireflies' light pulsed in the air, a steady reminder of the ancient power they had bound to themselves. And though the night was calm, Cassian knew that it would not stay that way for long.

Something was coming.

Chapter 43: The Arrival of the Luminaires

The Citadel was slowly coming back to life. Stone by stone, the outer walls were being repaired, and the cracks left by Tharion's darkness were beginning to fade. The fireflies' glow filled the air, their golden light soft and delicate, a beacon of hope as the siblings worked tirelessly to rebuild what had been lost.

But beneath that surface, Cassian could feel the weight of the ancient power still lingering. It was a quiet presence, always there, just below the surface, waiting. The fireflies' magic, though stronger than before, was now tied to something far more dangerous.

As the sun began to rise over the Citadel, casting a warm glow over the crumbling walls, Lyra appeared beside him, her flute hanging loosely at her side. Her expression was distant, her brow furrowed with worry.

"They'll be here soon," she said softly, her voice tinged with uncertainty.

Cassian knew what she meant. The Luminaires were on their way, summoned to help with the rebuilding and to lend their expertise in magic. But he could not shake the feeling that their arrival would complicate things. The fireflies' magic had changed—altered by the ancient power they had bound to it—and he was not sure how the Luminaires would react.

"They'll help us," Cassian said, though the tension in his voice was clear. "But we need to be careful. We are the ones who unlocked this power, and we cannot let them take control."

Orion, standing nearby, crossed his arms over his chest, his expression hard. "The Luminaires have always been our allies, but things are different now. We cannot trust that they will understand what we have done."

Lyra's eyes flickered with uncertainty. "They have always protected the fireflies' magic. They will see this change, and they might not accept it."

Eryndor, who had been listening quietly, stepped forward. His gaze was calm, but there was a weight in his eyes. "The Luminaires will sense the shift in the fireflies' magic the moment they arrive. They will know that something has changed—something profound. You must be prepared for questions."

Cassian swallowed hard. "And if they don't agree with what we've done?"

Eryndor's expression darkened. "Then you will have to defend your choices. The fireflies are bound to you now, to the magic you have unlocked. No one can take that away from you."

Orion's hand rested on the hilt of his sword, his stance tense. "If they try to take control, we'll stop them."

Cassian placed a hand on Orion's shoulder, calming him. "We need to keep this peaceful. We cannot afford to make enemies of the Luminaires. Not now."

As they spoke, the sound of footsteps echoed through the courtyard. Cassian turned to see a group of figures approaching the Citadel gates. The Luminaires had arrived, their robes shimmering with the faint glow of the fireflies' magic. At the head of the group was Master Evros, a stern-faced elder whose wisdom and strength had guided the Luminaires for decades.

The sight of the Luminaires should have brought relief, but instead, it only deepened the tension in the air. Cassian could see the flicker of surprise in their eyes as they stepped closer, sensing the shift in the fireflies' magic before any words were spoken.

"Cassian," Master Evros greeted, his voice calm but edged with something unreadable. "We came as soon as we received word. The fireflies' magic has... changed."

Cassian nodded, feeling the weight of the moment pressing down on him. "Yes. The fireflies' light has been restored, but in the process, we... we tapped into an ancient power buried deep within the Citadel."

Master Evros's eyes narrowed slightly. "An ancient power? And you bound this power to the fireflies?"

"Yes," Lyra said softly, stepping forward. "We did not have a choice. Tharion was destroying the Citadel, and the fireflies were fading. If we had not done it, everything would have been lost."

Evros exchanged a glance with the other Luminaires, his expression thoughtful. "You took a significant risk. The fireflies' magic has always been fragile, carefully balanced. To bind it to a force you do not fully understand—"

"We understand enough," Orion interrupted, his voice firm. "The power is under our control. The fireflies are stronger than ever."

Evros's gaze hardened. "Do you honestly believe that? Or is this power simply biding its time, waiting for the moment it can break free?"

Cassian felt his heart quicken. He had feared this moment—the moment when the Luminaires would question their decisions. And now, it was here. But he could not back down. The fireflies' magic was tied to them now, and they had to protect it.

"We're the ones who bound the power to the fireflies," Cassian said, his voice steady. "And we are the ones who will protect it. No one understands what happened better than we do."

Evros studied him for a long moment, the silence heavy. "This power you have unlocked—it is dangerous. It has changed the very nature of the Citadel and the fireflies themselves. You must be careful. If you lose control of it, there will be consequences."

Lyra's voice trembled slightly as she spoke. "We are doing everything we can to learn about it, to make sure it stays under control. That is why we need your help—to rebuild the Citadel and protect the fireflies."

Evros's expression softened, though his eyes still held a trace of wariness. "We will help you. But understand this—the fireflies' magic is no longer what it once was. You have awakened something far more powerful, and with that power comes significant risk."

Cassian nodded, though the tension in his chest did not ease. "We know the risks. And we will protect the Citadel, no matter what."

The Luminaires began to move through the courtyard, inspecting the damage and discussing the plans for rebuilding. But even as the work began, Cassian could feel the distance between them. The Luminaires were here to help, but they did not fully trust what the siblings had done. And Cassian could not blame them.

Eryndor approached Cassian, his gaze thoughtful. "You handled that well. But be cautious. The Luminaires will help, but they are wary of the power you have unlocked."

Cassian sighed, the weight of responsibility pressing down on him once more. "I know. But we did not have a choice."

"You made the right decision," Eryndor said softly. "But that doesn't mean it will be easy."

As the day wore on, the Luminaires worked alongside the siblings to begin rebuilding the Citadel. Stones were lifted, walls reinforced, and the fireflies' magic was used to stabilize the structure. But despite the progress, Cassian could feel the unspoken tension hanging in the air. The Luminaires did not fully trust them, and the siblings knew that their decisions would be under constant scrutiny.

That night, as the Citadel stood in the quiet glow of the fireflies, Cassian stood alone on the outer wall, looking out over the horizon. The ancient power they had bound to the fireflies was still there, waiting, pulsing just beneath the surface. He could feel it—a presence that was both awe-inspiring and terrifying.

Lyra appeared beside him, her voice quiet. "Do you think we can really control it? This power?"

Cassian did not answer immediately. Instead, he stared out at the darkness beyond the Citadel, feeling the weight of the ancient force pressing down on him.

"I don't know," he finally admitted. "But we don't have a choice."

As the fireflies flickered softly around them, Cassian knew that their battle was not over. They had saved the fireflies, but in doing so, they had unlocked something far more dangerous. And now, it was only a matter of time before others came looking for it.

Chapter 44: The Weight of Power

The Citadel's walls hummed with quiet energy as the fireflies flickered softly in the air, casting golden light over the newly reinforced stone. The Luminaires had been working tirelessly alongside the siblings to restore the Citadel, but despite the progress, an uneasy tension hung in the air.

Cassian stood at the center of the chamber where they had first harnessed the ancient power. His hands rested on the smooth surface of the tree-like structure that still pulsed faintly with energy. Though the fireflies' magic was bound to it, he could feel the wild force of the ancient power beneath, waiting. It was vast, uncontrollable, and the longer they held it, the more he realized how dangerous it was.

"We can't keep this," Lyra said softly from behind him. Her voice trembled with a mixture of fear and understanding. "This power... it's too much."

Cassian turned to her, his chest tightening at her words. He had been thinking the same thing but hearing her say it made it feel more real. The power they had bound to the fireflies had saved the Citadel, but it was not something they could control—not forever.

Orion entered the room, his sword hanging loosely at his side, his face lined with tension. "If we cannot control it, we have to destroy it. We cannot let this power fall into anyone else's hands."

Cassian's heart raced. Destroy it. The thought had crossed his mind more than once, but the idea terrified him. If they destroyed the power, would the fireflies' magic weaken? Would they lose the connection that had saved them from Tharion?

Eryndor stepped into the chamber, his gaze grave as he listened to their conversation. "Destroying the power might be the only way to ensure it doesn't overwhelm the fireflies—or worse, consume the Citadel itself."

Lyra's eyes filled with uncertainty. "But what happens to the fireflies if we do that? Will their magic survive without the connection?"

Eryndor's expression was somber. "The fireflies' magic was strong before you bound it to the ancient power. It can survive without it. But the question is whether you are willing to take that risk."

Cassian felt a knot of fear twist in his chest. The fireflies were everything—the light that had guided them, the magic that had saved them. But now, that light was tied to something far more dangerous, something they could barely control.

"We've already seen what happens when this power gets out of hand," Orion said, his voice low. "Tharion almost destroyed the Citadel, and if anyone else comes looking for this power, they could finish what he started."

Cassian's mind raced as he considered the possibility. Destroying the power might be the only way to protect the Citadel—and the world beyond—from those who would seek to control it. But doing so would weaken the fireflies, and the Citadel would never be the same.

"We have to think carefully about this," Cassian said, his voice heavy with the weight of the decision. "If we destroy the power, we might be protecting the Citadel, but we will also be losing something incredible. Something that has been part of this place for centuries."

Eryndor nodded solemnly. "That is the burden you carry now. This power is a force of both creation and destruction, and it cannot be wielded lightly. If you choose to destroy it, you will be choosing safety over potential. But if you keep it, you will always be at risk."

Lyra's face paled as she considered Eryndor's words. "And if we do not destroy it? What happens then?"

Eryndor's gaze darkened. "Then you will need to spend the rest of your lives guarding it, protecting it from those who would seek to use it for their own gain. It will be a burden that never ends."

Cassian felt the full weight of that reality pressing down on him. They had saved the Citadel, but at what cost? The ancient power they had tapped into was too dangerous for anyone to control. They could not keep it. Not forever.

"We can't live like this," Orion said, his voice firm. "Constantly guarding something that could destroy us. It is not sustainable."

Cassian knew his brother was right. The ancient power had been bound to the fireflies, but it was only a matter of time before someone else came looking for it. Tharion had been defeated, but there were others out there—those who would stop at nothing to take control of the Citadel's magic.

"We'll have to destroy it," Cassian said quietly, the words heavy on his tongue. "It's the only way to ensure the Citadel's safety."

Lyra's eyes filled with tears as she looked at him, her voice trembling. "But what if we lose the fireflies? What if their magic fades without the connection to the power?"

Cassian placed a hand on her shoulder, his voice filled with quiet determination. "The fireflies' light has always been their own. This power—it was never meant for them. We cannot risk losing everything just to hold on to something that is not ours to control."

Orion stepped forward, his stance resolute. "Then we do it. We destroy the power. It is the only way to protect the Citadel."

Eryndor's expression softened slightly, though his eyes remained grave. "You are making the right decision. But be warned—destroying the power will not be easy. It has been bound to the fireflies and separating them could be dangerous."

Cassian nodded, the weight of the decision pressing down on him like a stone. "We do not have a choice. We cannot let this power destroy us."

As the siblings stood together, united in their decision, the fireflies' light flickered softly around them, their golden glow fragile but unwavering. The ancient power pulsed faintly beneath the surface, as if sensing their intent.

"We'll find a way," Cassian said, his voice filled with quiet determination. "We will destroy the power, and we will protect the fireflies. No matter what it takes."

Eryndor nodded, his expression filled with both respect and concern. "Then we must prepare. Destroying a power like this will require more than strength—it will require understanding. We will need to find the source of its connection to the fireflies, and only then can we sever it."

Cassian's heart raced as he thought about what lay ahead. Destroying the power would not be simple, and the risk of losing the fireflies was real. But it was a risk they had to take.

"We'll do whatever it takes," Cassian said, his voice steady. "We'll protect the Citadel, even if it means giving up this power."

The fireflies flickered in the air, their light soft and fragile, as the siblings prepared for the next stage of their journey. The decision had been made. The ancient power was too much for anyone to control.

And now, they would destroy it—before it destroyed them.

Chapter 45: The First Step Toward Destruction

The Citadel stood quietly under the weight of the decision. The fireflies' soft glow filled the air as if they, too, sensed the gravity of what was to come. Cassian stood in the center of the chamber, his hands resting on the ancient, tree-like structure that pulsed with faint energy. The power that had saved them, that had restored the fireflies' light, now felt like a ticking clock—one that they had no choice but to stop.

Orion, always the protector, paced the room, his hand resting on the hilt of his sword. "So how do we do this? We have agreed to destroy the power, but what is the first step? How do we even begin to unravel something this big?"

Eryndor, who stood quietly by the entrance, nodded thoughtfully. "This power is old, older than the Citadel itself. It is woven deeply into the fireflies' magic now, and separating the two will not be simple. We will need to find the source of its connection."

Lyra stepped forward, her face pale with worry. "What if we lose the fireflies in the process? What if we cannot separate them from the power without destroying their magic entirely?"

Cassian's heart clenched at the thought. The fireflies were everything—the light of the Citadel, the very heart of its magic. Losing them would mean losing the very essence of what they had fought to protect.

"We have to trust that the fireflies can survive without this power," Cassian said quietly, though the uncertainty in his voice was clear.

"Their magic was strong before we tapped into the ancient force. We have to believe that it will be strong again once we free them."

Eryndor stepped closer to the ancient tree-like structure, his gaze focused on the faint pulsing of energy that radiated from it. "The key to severing the connection lies deep within the Citadel—beneath this very structure. The power is bound here, at the heart of the Citadel's magic. If we can reach the source of that binding, we can begin the process of unraveling it."

Orion stopped pacing, his brow furrowed. "You are saying we have to go deeper? Into the foundations of the Citadel?"

Eryndor nodded, his expression grave. "Yes. There is an ancient chamber beneath this one, hidden for centuries. It was where the fireflies' magic was first tied to the Citadel, and it is there that we will find the answers we need."

Cassian's pulse quickened. The idea of venturing deeper into the Citadel, into a place that had been hidden for so long, filled him with both fear and a strange sense of purpose. The Citadel had always been a place of mystery, and now they were about to uncover one of its oldest secrets.

"We'll need to prepare," Cassian said, his voice steady. "This isn't going to be easy."

Lyra nodded, though her face was still lined with worry. "And once we find this chamber? How do we sever the connection without destroying the fireflies?"

Eryndor's eyes darkened. "That is the challenge. The fireflies' magic is tied to the ancient power now and separating them could weaken both. But we have no choice. If we do not act, the power will consume everything."

Orion clenched his fists, his voice hard. "Then let us do this. The longer we wait, the more dangerous this power becomes."

Cassian took a deep breath, his mind racing. They were about to take the first step toward destroying something that had been part of the Citadel for centuries. It felt monumental, terrifying—but necessary.

"We'll gather what we need," Cassian said. "We'll be ready."

The journey into the depths of the Citadel began as the sun began to set, casting long shadows over the crumbling stone walls. Cassian, Lyra, and Orion, along with Eryndor, moved through the darkened halls with a sense of quiet determination. The fireflies fluttered around them, their golden light soft but unwavering, guiding them as they descended into the lower levels.

The deeper they went, the colder the air became. The ancient stone walls seemed to press in around them, and the quiet hum of the fireflies' magic felt distant, fragile. Cassian's pulse quickened as they reached a narrow passageway, hidden behind a broken pillar, which led even further down into the Citadel's foundations.

"This is the entrance to the ancient chamber," Eryndor said quietly, his voice barely more than a whisper. "It has been sealed for centuries, but now... it is time to open it."

Lyra hesitated, her hand gripping her flute tightly. "What if we can't control what we find down there?"

Cassian placed a hand on her shoulder, his voice soft but filled with resolve. "We will face it together. Whatever it takes."

With that, they stepped into the passageway, their footsteps echoing through the narrow corridor as they descended deeper into the heart of the Citadel. The air grew colder still, and the walls seemed to hum with a faint, pulsing energy—the same energy that had radiated from the tree-like structure in the upper chamber.

After what felt like hours, they reached a large, circular stone door. Ancient runes, long faded but still faintly glowing, covered its surface, and the air around it thrummed with the same wild energy they had felt when they first tapped into the ancient power.

"This is it," Eryndor said, his voice low. "The ancient chamber where the fireflies' magic was first tied to the Citadel."

Cassian stepped forward, his heart pounding as he placed his hand on the door. The stone was cold beneath his fingers, and for a moment, he felt a strange connection—a pull, as if the door itself was waiting for him to open it.

"We're ready," he said softly.

Eryndor nodded, and with a quiet murmur of ancient words, the runes on the door flared to life. The stone groaned as it slowly began to shift, revealing a dark, cavernous space beyond.

The moment the door opened, a surge of energy rushed toward them, powerful and wild. The fireflies' light flickered, their golden glow struggling to hold back the darkness that seemed to press in from the chamber beyond.

Cassian took a deep breath, his pulse quickening as they stepped into the ancient chamber. The walls were covered in more runes, glowing faintly with the same energy they had felt above. At the center of the room, a massive stone altar stood, radiating a powerful, pulsing light.

"This is the source," Eryndor said, his voice filled with reverence. "The place where the fireflies' magic was first bound to the Citadel."

Orion stepped forward, his expression tense. "And this is where we sever it."

Cassian's heart raced as he stared at the altar. The power that had saved the Citadel, the force that had restored the fireflies' magic, was here, waiting. But it was also the power that threatened to destroy everything if they did not act.

"We can do this," Cassian said, his voice steady. "We have to."

As they approached the altar, the fireflies' light flared brighter, as if sensing the importance of the moment. The ancient power pulsed beneath them, wild and dangerous, but for the first time, Cassian felt a strange sense of calm.

They had come this far. And now, they would finish what they had started.

"We'll sever the connection," Cassian whispered. "And we'll save the Citadel."

Chapter 46: The Severing

The ancient chamber thrummed with an energy that seemed to pulse from the very walls. Cassian could feel it in his bones—the wild, untamed power that had been bound to the fireflies' magic. The room was vast, illuminated by the faint glow of ancient runes that had lain dormant for centuries, waiting for this moment.

The altar at the center of the chamber pulsed with a soft, rhythmic light, its glow mirroring the fireflies' delicate dance above. Cassian, Lyra, Orion, and Eryndor stood in a quiet circle around the altar, each of them feeling the immense weight of what was about to happen.

"This is the heart of the power," Eryndor said quietly, his voice barely more than a whisper. "It is here that the fireflies were first bound to the Citadel's magic. And it is here that we must sever that bond."

Lyra's hands trembled as she held her flute, her eyes wide with fear and uncertainty. "What if we cannot do it? What if the power is too strong?"

Cassian placed a steadying hand on her shoulder, his voice calm but firm. "We do not have a choice. If we do not act, this power will consume everything. We have to trust that the fireflies will survive."

Orion's grip tightened on the hilt of his sword, his expression hard. "We need to act fast. The longer we wait, the more unstable this power becomes."

Eryndor nodded, his gaze locked on the altar. "This will not be easy. The fireflies' magic is tied to this power now and separating them will be dangerous. But if we do nothing, the consequences will be far worse."

Cassian took a deep breath, his heart pounding in his chest. He could feel the ancient power swirling around them, vast and unknowable, but he also felt the fireflies' light—a fragile but resilient force that had guided them through so much. They had to believe that the fireflies could survive this.

"We'll do this together," Cassian said, his voice filled with quiet determination. "We've come this far—we can't stop now."

Eryndor stepped forward, raising his hands as he began to chant softly in a language Cassian did not fully understand. The runes on the altar glowed brighter, responding to the magic that filled the room. The air seemed to thicken with energy, and Cassian could feel the power of the altar building, pulsing in time with the fireflies' light.

Lyra lifted her flute to her lips, her hands shaking slightly as she began to play a slow, haunting melody. The fireflies fluttered in response, their golden light intensifying as they danced above the altar, their magic intertwining with the ancient power.

Cassian stepped closer to the altar, his heart racing as he felt the weight of the power pressing down on him. The energy in the room was growing stronger, more volatile, and he knew that they were nearing the moment of truth.

"Now," Eryndor said, his voice filled with urgency. "You must focus on the fireflies—on their light. You are the ones who bound them to this power, and only you can sever that bond."

Cassian nodded, his gaze locked on the altar. The fireflies' light flickered above him, their golden glow fragile but steady. He reached out, placing his hand on the altar's surface, feeling the cold stone beneath his fingers. The power surged through him, wild and dangerous, but he held on, focusing on the fireflies' light—their magic, their essence.

Lyra's melody filled the air, weaving through the ancient chamber like a thread of light. The fireflies responded, their glow brightening, their magic intertwining with the music as they fluttered around the altar.

Orion stepped forward, his sword in hand, his eyes filled with resolve. "We'll protect the fireflies, no matter what happens."

Cassian's heart pounded as he closed his eyes, focusing all his energy on the fireflies. He could feel the ancient power fighting back, resisting the separation, but he knew that they had to do this. They had to sever the connection before the power consumed everything.

The runes on the walls flared with light, and the altar pulsed violently, sending a shockwave of energy through the room. Cassian staggered, his hands gripping the altar as the power surged through him, overwhelming and chaotic.

"We're losing control!" Lyra cried, her voice filled with panic.

Eryndor's voice rose above the chaos, his chant growing louder, more insistent. "Focus on the fireflies! You must concentrate—now!"

Cassian gritted his teeth, his mind racing as he fought to regain control. The power was pulling at him, tempting him to give in, but he forced himself to focus on the fireflies—their light, their magic. He could feel their presence, fragile but determined, pushing back against the ancient force.

"We can do this," Cassian whispered, his voice trembling with effort. "We have to."

Lyra's melody shifted, becoming more urgent, more powerful. The fireflies' light flared, bright and brilliant, filling the chamber with golden warmth. Cassian could feel their magic pushing back against the ancient power, resisting the bond that had been forced upon them.

Orion stepped forward, his sword glowing with the fireflies' light. "We will not let this power destroy us. We are stronger than it."

With a final surge of effort, Cassian pushed all his energy into the fireflies' light, focusing on the bond they shared. He could feel the power of the altar weakening, its hold on the fireflies beginning to slip.

The chamber shook as the energy built to a crescendo, the ancient power raging against the separation. The runes on the walls flared violently, their light flickering, as if the very foundation of the Citadel were about to collapse.

But then, in a sudden flash of brilliant light, the power broke.

The energy that had filled the room dissipated in an instant, and the air fell still. The fireflies fluttered softly around them, their golden light pulsing gently in the silence. The altar's glow faded, its power severed from the fireflies.

Cassian staggered back, gasping for breath, his body trembling with exhaustion. Lyra's flute fell silent, and she collapsed to her knees, her face pale and drenched in sweat.

Orion lowered his sword, his chest heaving as he stared at the now-dormant altar. "Did we... did we do it?"

Eryndor stepped forward, his eyes scanning the room. The runes on the walls had dimmed, their power spent, and the ancient energy that had once filled the chamber was gone.

"Yes," Eryndor said quietly, his voice filled with awe. "You have done it. The bond has been severed."

Cassian looked up at the fireflies, their light still flickering softly in the air. The connection to the ancient power was gone, but the fireflies remained—fragile, but alive.

"We did it," Cassian whispered, his voice filled with relief. "We saved the fireflies."

Lyra wiped her brow, her eyes filled with tears. "I was so afraid... that we'd lose them."

Orion placed a hand on her shoulder, his expression softening. "We did not. They are still with us."

Eryndor nodded, his gaze thoughtful. "The ancient power has been severed, but the fireflies' magic endures. You have made the right choice."

Cassian took a deep breath, the weight of their victory settling over him. They had done it. The ancient power that had threatened to consume the Citadel was gone, and the fireflies were safe.

But as they stood in the quiet chamber, Cassian could not shake the feeling that their journey was far from over. The fireflies' magic had survived, but it had been changed by the ancient power, and there were still many questions left unanswered.

"We'll rebuild," Cassian said softly, his voice filled with quiet determination. "And we'll protect the fireflies—no matter what."

Lyra and Orion nodded in agreement, their bond stronger than ever. They had faced the impossible and emerged victorious, but the future of the Citadel was still uncertain.

As the fireflies fluttered around them, their golden light a beacon of hope, Cassian knew that their journey had only just begun.

Chapter 47: The Cost of Victory

The chamber was silent, save for the soft hum of the fireflies as they fluttered above. The golden light that had once felt fragile now seemed steady, but there was an undeniable shift in the air. The energy of the ancient power was gone, but in its absence, Cassian felt a strange void—a hollow space where that wild, untamed force had once pulsed.

Cassian stood beside the altar, his hands still trembling from the exertion of severing the bond between the fireflies and the ancient power. His breath came in shallow bursts as he glanced at his siblings. Lyra was kneeling, her hands resting on the cold stone floor, her face pale with exhaustion. Orion, though still standing, had a distant look in his eyes, as if the weight of what they had done had not fully settled yet.

"We did it," Cassian said, his voice barely more than a whisper. "We saved the fireflies."

Lyra lifted her gaze to the fireflies above, their soft glow lighting up the chamber in warm, golden hues. "But at what cost? The fireflies... they feel different."

Cassian knew what she meant. The fireflies' light, though still present, had lost some of the intensity it once had. It was as if severing the bond with the ancient power had taken something from them, leaving them diminished, though not entirely broken.

"They're still here," Orion said, though his voice lacked the usual certainty. "That is what matters. They survived."

Eryndor stepped forward, his expression thoughtful as he surveyed the chamber. The runes on the walls had faded into darkness, and

249

the altar that had once pulsed with ancient energy was now cold and lifeless. "You have done what needed to be done. The ancient power was too dangerous to keep, and now the Citadel is free from its influence."

Cassian nodded, but he could not shake the unease settling in his chest. The ancient power was gone, but the fireflies' magic felt weaker, less vibrant. The Citadel, once brimming with energy, now seemed quieter, more fragile.

"We need to get back to the surface," Cassian said, turning to his siblings. "There's still work to be done."

Lyra stood slowly, her legs shaking as she regained her balance. "Do you think the Luminaires will understand what we have done? They might see the fireflies' magic weakening and think we made a mistake."

Orion's jaw tightened. "Let them question us. We did what we had to do. No one can control that kind of power."

Eryndor's eyes darkened slightly. "You are right to be cautious. The Luminaires will sense the change in the fireflies' magic, and they may not agree with your decision to sever the bond. But you must stand by it. The fireflies' magic is still theirs, still pure. And over time, it will strengthen again."

Cassian felt a flicker of hope at Eryndor's words, though the uncertainty still lingered. The fireflies had been tied to the ancient power for so long, and now, without it, their future felt more fragile than ever.

"We'll face whatever comes," Cassian said, his voice steady. "Together."

With that, they began the slow ascent back to the surface. The dark, narrow passageways seemed even colder and more desolate than before, but the fireflies' light guided them, soft but unwavering. Cassian could feel the weight of the Citadel above them—the ancient structure that had stood for centuries, now altered by their actions.

When they finally reached the main courtyard, the sight that greeted them was both familiar and strange. The Citadel's stone walls had been reinforced by the Luminaires, but there was an undeniable sense of something missing. The fireflies, once the brightest part of the Citadel's magic, now flickered with a quieter, more subdued light.

The Luminaires, who had been waiting anxiously for their return, approached them with wary eyes. Master Evros, the leader of the Luminaires, stepped forward, his expression unreadable as he looked at Cassian, Lyra, and Orion.

"You have returned," Evros said, his voice calm but filled with an edge of uncertainty. "But something has changed. The fireflies... their magic feels different."

Cassian exchanged a glance with his siblings before answering. "We severed their connection to the ancient power that had bound them. It was too dangerous to keep. We could not risk the Citadel being consumed by it."

Evros's eyes narrowed, though his tone remained measured. "You severed the bond? And in doing so, you have weakened the fireflies' magic."

"We had no choice," Orion said, his voice firm. "That power was unstable. If we had kept it, the fireflies would have been destroyed."

Lyra stepped forward, her voice softer but filled with resolve. "The fireflies survived. That is what matters. Their light may be weaker now, but it will grow stronger again in time."

Evros studied them for a long moment, his expression unreadable. The other Luminaires stood behind him, their eyes filled with uncertainty as they glanced at the flickering fireflies above.

"You made a difficult decision," Evros finally said, his voice heavy with the weight of their actions. "One that will change the Citadel forever. The fireflies' magic will need time to recover, but I hope you understand that this could have lasting consequences."

Cassian felt the knot of fear tighten in his chest. He had known there would be consequences but hearing them spoken aloud made them feel more real. The Citadel, once a place of great magical power, was now weakened. The fireflies, though still alive, were no longer the same force they had once been.

"We understand," Cassian said, his voice quiet but resolute. "But we could not let that power remain. It was too much for anyone to control."

Evros nodded slowly, his gaze softening slightly. "You did what you believed was right. And for that, you have my respect. But the road ahead will not be easy. The fireflies will need protection now more than ever, especially in their weakened state."

Orion's hand rested on the hilt of his sword. "We will protect them. No matter what."

Lyra glanced at Cassian, her eyes filled with quiet determination. "We have been through worse. We can do this."

Cassian took a deep breath, feeling the weight of their decision settle over him like a heavy cloak. The Citadel was safe, for now, but the fireflies were vulnerable. And though the ancient power was gone, there would always be those who sought to control the fireflies' magic.

"We'll rebuild," Cassian said softly, his voice filled with quiet resolve. "And we'll protect the fireflies—together."

As the fireflies flickered softly above, their golden light a reminder of all that had been sacrificed, Cassian knew that their journey was far from over. They had saved the fireflies, but the cost had been great. And the future of the Citadel, though uncertain, was still in their hands.

Chapter 48: A Fragile Future

The fireflies' soft glow flickered in the twilight, casting long shadows across the Citadel's ancient stone walls. The once vibrant magic that had filled the air was now quieter, more subdued, though the warmth of the fireflies' light still lingered. The Citadel had been saved, but Cassian could feel that their victory had come at a cost.

Cassian stood at the edge of the main courtyard, his eyes scanning the horizon. The Luminaires were scattered throughout the Citadel, their hands and magic aiding in the final stages of restoration. The walls were stronger now, the physical damage repaired, but the deeper scars left by the severing of the ancient power were not so easily mended.

Lyra approached quietly, her face thoughtful as she watched the fireflies dance above them. "They've changed," she said softly. "I can feel it in their light. It is not as strong as it once was."

Cassian nodded, his chest tightening at her words. "I know. But they are still here. They are still with us."

Orion joined them, his gaze hard as he looked up at the flickering fireflies. "We did what we had to do. We made the right call. That power... it was not meant for anyone."

Cassian's mind drifted to the ancient chamber below, where the wild, untamed force had once pulsed with energy. Now, that power was gone, severed from the fireflies forever. But its absence left a hollow space—a lingering uncertainty about what would come next.

Eryndor approached, his presence as steady and reassuring as ever. His expression was calm, but there was a quiet gravity in his eyes. "The Citadel will recover. The fireflies' light, though weakened, will grow stronger again in time. But you must remain vigilant. There are still forces in the world who seek power, and they will not stop simply because you have severed this one."

Cassian felt a cold knot of unease twist in his chest. The fireflies, in their weakened state, were vulnerable. Though the ancient power had been destroyed, the Citadel was still a beacon of magic, and there were others who would seek to control it.

"What happens now?" Lyra asked, her voice filled with uncertainty. "Are we safe?"

Eryndor shook his head slowly. "No place of magic is ever truly safe. The fireflies' light will always draw attention. There are those who will see the Citadel as a place of power, and now that its defenses are weakened, it may attract new threats."

Orion's jaw tightened. "Then we will make sure it is protected. We have faced worse. Whatever comes next, we will be ready."

Cassian nodded, though the weight of Eryndor's words settled heavily over him. They had spent their entire lives protecting the fireflies, but now, the challenges ahead felt more uncertain than ever. The ancient power had been a threat, but it had also been a part of the Citadel for centuries. Its absence created a void, one that others might try to fill.

"We'll rebuild the Citadel," Cassian said, his voice filled with quiet determination. "And we'll protect the fireflies, no matter what it takes."

Eryndor placed a hand on Cassian's shoulder, his gaze filled with quiet respect. "You have proven yourselves as guardians of the fireflies, but your journey is far from over. The Citadel's future rests in your hands now. And as long as the fireflies still flicker, there will always be those who seek their magic."

Lyra glanced at Cassian, her eyes filled with both hope and fear. "Do you think the fireflies will ever be as strong as they once were?"

Cassian hesitated before answering. "I do not know. But we will help them grow. We will find a way."

Orion's hand rested on the hilt of his sword, his expression resolute. "Whatever comes, we'll face it together."

As they stood in the fading light, the fireflies danced softly above them, their glow a fragile but constant reminder of all that had been fought for and won. The Citadel was safe—for now. But Cassian knew that their journey was far from over. The world was vast, and the forces of darkness, greed, and ambition would always linger on the horizon.

"We've come this far," Cassian said softly, his voice filled with quiet resolve. "And we'll keep going."

Eryndor nodded, his expression solemn. "You have the strength and wisdom to lead the Citadel into a new era. But be prepared—for the future is uncertain, and the challenges you face will only grow more complex."

Cassian felt the weight of those words, but he also felt a flicker of hope. They had faced the ancient power and survived. They had protected the fireflies through darkness and danger, and they would continue to protect them, no matter what came next.

As the fireflies' light flickered softly in the evening sky, Cassian knew that the road ahead would be difficult. There would be new threats, new challenges, and new mysteries to uncover. But for now, they had each other, and that was enough.

The Citadel, though changed, still stood strong.

And as long as the fireflies' light continued to glow, there was hope for the future.

Chapter 49: Rebuilding the Light

The wind carried a cool breeze through the Citadel's courtyard as Cassian stood at the edge of the main gates, watching as the last rays of the sun dipped below the horizon. The Citadel, though bruised and weakened by the battles they had fought, still stood proud. Its stone walls had been fortified, the cracks mended, and the Luminaires were hard at work, doing what they could to restore the Citadel's magical defenses.

But Cassian knew that the real work had only just begun.

The fireflies' light, though still present, flickered faintly in the twilight, casting a soft glow over the courtyard. It was a reminder of all they had sacrificed and all that remained uncertain. The fireflies had survived, but their magic was weaker now, and it would take time to rebuild the strength they had once known.

Lyra stood beside him, her flute resting gently at her side. She had been playing softly throughout the day, coaxing the fireflies to gather their energy, to heal. But even she could feel the difference in their light.

"They're struggling," she said quietly, her eyes filled with concern. "It's like they're trying to hold on, but something is missing."

Cassian nodded, his chest heavy with the weight of her words. "They have been through so much. We severed them from a power they were bound to for centuries. It is going to take time for them to recover."

Orion joined them, his sword resting on his back, his eyes scanning the horizon. He had always been the protector, and now, more than ever, Cassian could see the tension in his posture—the constant readiness to defend what they had fought so hard to save.

"The Citadel is vulnerable," Orion said, his voice low but firm. "We've done what we can to strengthen the walls, but without the fireflies at full strength, we're still at risk."

Cassian knew he was right. The Citadel, even in its most fortified state, was only as strong as the magic that protected it. And the fireflies, though resilient, were different from they had been before the bond with the ancient power had been severed.

"We'll rebuild," Cassian said, his voice filled with quiet determination. "We'll help the fireflies heal, and we'll make sure the Citadel is protected—no matter what it takes."

Eryndor approached, his expression thoughtful as he looked out over the Citadel. "The fireflies will grow stronger in time," he said softly. "But you must remember that their magic is now purely their own. It is no longer tied to anything outside of them. That makes them vulnerable, but also pure."

Lyra glanced at Eryndor, her brow furrowed. "Do you think we made the right choice? Severing them from the ancient power?"

Eryndor smiled faintly, though his eyes held a quiet sadness. "It was the only choice you could have made. That power was never meant for the fireflies and keeping them bound to it would have destroyed them in the end. You did what was necessary, and now the fireflies have a chance to recover—on their own terms."

Cassian felt a flicker of relief at Eryndor's words, but the uncertainty still lingered. The fireflies' light had always been a symbol of hope, of protection. Now, that light was fragile, and the world around them was filled with dangers they could not yet see.

"We need to be prepared for what comes next," Orion said, his voice edged with tension. "We've dealt with Tharion, but there will always be others—those who want to control the fireflies' magic, especially now that it's unbound."

Cassian knew that was true. The Citadel had always been a beacon of magic, and even without the ancient power, there would be those who sought to take control of it. The weakened state of the fireflies would only make them more vulnerable to outside threats.

"We'll protect them," Cassian said, his voice firm. "We've done it before, and we'll do it again."

Lyra smiled faintly, though her eyes were filled with both hope and worry. "We are stronger together. We have always been able to face whatever comes."

Eryndor nodded, his expression thoughtful. "The fireflies are resilient, but so are you. You have proven yourselves as guardians of this place but remember—the Citadel's future is not just about defending it from outside threats. It is about rebuilding, restoring the magic that has always been here."

Cassian took a deep breath, feeling the weight of those words. The fireflies had always been at the heart of the Citadel, and now, more than ever, they needed to focus on helping them heal. But the thought of future threats, of forces they could not yet see, lingered at the back of his mind.

"We'll rebuild the Citadel," Cassian said softly. "And we will rebuild the fireflies' light. But we cannot do it alone."

Orion crossed his arms, his face set with determination. "We have the Luminaires on our side, and we have faced worse before. Whatever comes, we will be ready."

Lyra placed a hand on Cassian's shoulder, her voice filled with quiet resolve. "We will take it one step at a time. The fireflies will heal, and we will be here for them—always."

Cassian felt a flicker of hope as he looked at his siblings. They had been through so much together—faced impossible odds, fought against darkness, and saved the fireflies from destruction. And though the future remained uncertain, he knew that as long as they stood together, they could face whatever came next.

But as the fireflies flickered softly above, their light fragile and delicate, Cassian could not shake the feeling that something else was waiting—just beyond the horizon. The Citadel had been saved, but the world outside was vast and filled with unknown dangers.

"We'll be ready," Cassian said softly, his voice filled with quiet determination. "No matter what comes, we'll protect this place."

The fireflies danced softly in the fading light, their glow a fragile reminder of all that had been fought for and won. But even as their light flickered, there was a sense of hope—a belief that the fireflies would grow stronger, that the Citadel would endure.

And though the road ahead was uncertain, Cassian knew one thing for sure:

Their journey was far from over.

Chapter 50: A Light in the Darkness

The night sky stretched above the Citadel, clear and quiet, with a scattering of stars twinkling in the distance. The fireflies danced softly in the air, their glow weaker than it had once been, but still present—a reminder that even in darkness, there was light. The Citadel, though scarred by the battles they had fought, stood strong, a beacon of resilience.

Cassian stood on the edge of the Citadel's outer wall, his gaze sweeping across the horizon. The cool breeze tugged at his cloak as he watched the fireflies flicker in the distance. The air was filled with the sounds of quiet rebuilding—Luminaires and workers reinforcing the final sections of the walls, while others gathered near the central courtyard, talking in hushed tones about the future.

Lyra joined him, her presence calm and reassuring as she leaned against the stone wall. Her flute was tucked away, but Cassian could still hear the echoes of the melodies she had played to guide the fireflies, to help them heal. It had been a long, arduous journey, and though they had survived, the weight of their decisions lingered.

"Do you think we've done enough?" Lyra asked quietly, her voice filled with uncertainty. "The fireflies... they're still so fragile."

Cassian sighed, the tension of the past few weeks weighing heavily on his shoulders. "We have done everything we could. The fireflies survived, and now it is up to us to help them recover. It is not going to be easy, but we will get there."

Orion approached from behind, his usual quiet strength evident as he stood beside them. "We have faced worse. The fireflies are still here, and as long as they are, the Citadel will stand."

Cassian nodded, though the uncertainty still clung to him. They had saved the fireflies, severed the bond with the ancient power, and restored the Citadel's walls. But in doing so, they had weakened the fireflies' magic, and the Citadel felt more vulnerable than ever before.

Eryndor appeared behind them, his steps quiet but sure as he joined their silent vigil. His presence had been a constant through all of this, and Cassian found comfort in his calm, steady wisdom. The fireflies fluttered around Eryndor as if drawn to him, their light flickering softly in the night air.

"The Citadel will heal," Eryndor said quietly, his voice filled with quiet conviction. "But healing takes time. The fireflies will grow stronger, and so will you."

Cassian looked out over the landscape, the darkness stretching far beyond the Citadel walls. The world outside was vast, and though they had defeated Tharion and severed the ancient power, he could not shake the feeling that their challenges were far from over.

"There's something out there," Cassian said softly, his voice filled with quiet concern. "Something waiting. I can feel it."

Eryndor nodded slowly. "You are right to feel that way. The world is filled with forces that seek power, and the fireflies' magic, even in its weakened state, will always attract attention. You must remain vigilant."

Lyra's brow furrowed as she glanced at Cassian. "Do you think we will be ready? For whatever comes next?"

Cassian smiled faintly, though the weight of the unknown still pressed on him. "We will face it. Whatever it is, we will be ready."

Orion's hand rested on the hilt of his sword, his gaze scanning the horizon. "We have always been ready. Whatever comes, we will protect this place."

Eryndor placed a hand on Cassian's shoulder, his expression filled with quiet pride. "You have all shown great strength and wisdom. You have proven that the Citadel, and the fireflies, are in capable hands. But remember, this is only the beginning. The world is ever-changing, and the challenges you face will continue to evolve."

Cassian nodded, feeling a strange sense of both hope and trepidation. The Citadel had been saved, but there was no telling what lay ahead. The fireflies were fragile, their magic no longer bound to the ancient power, and the world outside was filled with unknown forces. But as long as they stood together, Cassian believed they could face whatever came next.

The stars twinkled above, their light distant but constant, a reminder that the world was vast and filled with possibilities. The fireflies' glow, though faint, still flickered with hope, and Cassian knew that as long as the fireflies' light remained, there would always be a path forward.

"We'll rebuild," Cassian said softly, his voice filled with quiet determination. "We'll help the fireflies grow stronger, and we'll protect the Citadel."

Lyra smiled, her eyes filled with a quiet, unwavering belief. "We have made it this far. We will keep going."

Orion's expression softened, his hand resting on the stone wall as he looked out at the Citadel, they had fought so hard to protect. "Together."

As the fireflies flickered in the soft night air, their light a beacon of hope, Cassian felt a sense of peace settle over him. The road ahead was uncertain, but for the first time in weeks, he felt a sense of quiet confidence.

They had faced impossible odds, fought against darkness, and saved the fireflies from destruction. But there was still so much more to do, so much more to protect.

The Citadel stood strong, its walls rebuilt, its magic still flickering. And though the future remained uncertain, Cassian knew one thing for sure:

Their story was far from over.

As the fireflies danced softly above them, their golden light filling the night with a sense of quiet hope, Cassian allowed himself to believe in the future they were building—a future where the fireflies would shine brightly again.

And as long as that light remained, there was always hope.

Epilogue: A New Dawn

AS DAWN BROKE OVER the Citadel, the first rays of sunlight spilled across the courtyard, illuminating the stone walls that had been carefully restored. The fireflies danced softly in the early morning light, their glow now vibrant and warm, a testament to the healing they had undergone since the severing of the ancient power.

Cassian stood at the edge of the courtyard, watching as the Luminaires worked alongside the villagers to further strengthen the Citadel's defenses. The air was filled with laughter and chatter, a sense of community flourishing amidst the remnants of what had once been a place of despair.

Lyra approached, her flute in hand, a soft smile gracing her lips. "The fireflies seem to be growing stronger each day," she said, her eyes sparkling with renewed hope. "It's like they're finding their light again."

Cassian nodded, his heart swelling with pride. "They have always had that light within them. It just took a little time to find it again after everything we went through."

Orion joined them, his expression serious yet filled with a quiet resolve. "We have built a solid foundation here, but we cannot let our guard down. The world outside is still full of uncertainties."

Eryndor walked over, his presence calm and steady as always. "You are wise to remain vigilant. The fireflies may have regained their strength, but the magic of the Citadel is still a beacon to those who would seek to exploit it."

Cassian turned to face the horizon, a mixture of determination and apprehension in his heart. "We will always protect it. This place is more than just a sanctuary for the fireflies—it is our home. We have fought for it, and we will continue to fight for its future."

As the sun climbed higher, casting a warm glow over the Citadel, Cassian felt a sense of renewal wash over him. The challenges they had faced had forged a bond between them, one that would withstand whatever came next.

In the distance, he could see the outline of the forest where the fireflies had first danced under the moonlight, a place of magic and mystery that still held many secrets. It was a reminder that their journey was far from over, and there were still stories to be written, adventures to be had.

As the fireflies flickered around him, their light now a symbol of hope, Cassian knew that their tale was only beginning. The bonds of family and friendship had been strengthened through trials, and together, they would face whatever challenges lay ahead.

With a smile, he turned back to his siblings, feeling the warmth of the sun on his face. "Let us get to work. There is still so much to do, and I cannot wait to see what the future holds for all of us."

As they moved forward, united in purpose and filled with hope, the Citadel stood strong, its walls alive with the magic of the fireflies, a promise of light in the ever-looming darkness.

And so, the legacy of the fireflies continued, their light illuminating the path ahead, guiding them toward a future filled with endless possibilities.

As they moved forward, united in purpose and filled with hope, the Citadel stood strong, its walls alive with the magic of the fireflies, a promise of light in the ever-looming darkness.

And so, the legacy of the fireflies continued, their light illuminating the path ahead, guiding them toward a future filled with endless possibilities.

The End?

Don't miss out!

Visit the website below and you can sign up to receive emails whenever Night Intruder publishes a new book. There's no charge and no obligation.

https://books2read.com/r/B-A-GDRMC-UGIDF

BOOKS 2 READ

Connecting independent readers to independent writers.

Also by Night Intruder

Fading Ecoes
Fading Echoes: Stories Of Love And Loss Volume 1

Firefies Of The Heart
Shadows Of The Fireflies
Echoes Of The Fireflies:The Citadel

Fireflies Of The Heart
Fireflies Of The Heart

Fragments of Grace and Dreams Book Of Poems Volume 1
Fragments of Grace and Dreams Book Of Poems Volume 1

Phantoms Breath
Phantom's Breath Volume 1
Phantom's Breath Elara's Veil Volume 2

About the Author

Night Intruder is a passionate storyteller and poet who finds inspiration in the beauty of nature and the complexities of the human experience. With a deep love for fantasy and magical realism, he weaves tales that explore love, loss, and the mysteries that bind us all.

Living in Ocala, Florida, Night Intruder spends his days surrounded by the wonders of the world, always on the lookout for inspiration in the everyday moments of life.